ME *and* BILLY

ME and BILLY

James Lincoln Collier

MARSHALL CAVENDISH
New York • London • Singapore

Text copyright © 2004 by James Lincoln Collier
Marshall Cavendish, 99 White Plains Road, Tarrytown, NY 10591
www.marshallcavendish.com

Library of Congress Cataloging-in-Publication Data
Collier, James Lincoln, 1928-
Me and Billy / James Lincoln Collier.— 1st ed.
p. cm.
Summary: After escaping the orphanage where they have spent their lives together,
two boys become assistants to a con artist, and while Possum objects to the lying,
stealing, and cheating, Billy only cares about making money and taking life easy.

ISBN 0-7614-5174-9

[1. Swindlers and swindling—Fiction. 2. Orphans—Fiction. 3. Runaways—Fiction.
4. Best friends—Fiction. 5. Friendship—Fiction. 6. Conduct of life—Fiction.] I.
Title.
PZ7.C678Me 2004
[Fic]—dc22
2003026865
The text of this book is set in Goudy.
Book design by Patrice Sheridan
Printed in the United States of America
First edition
1   3   5   6   4   2

For Harry

Chapter One

Me and Billy liked to get Cook to talk about how things were on the outside, beyond the high brick wall that went around the Home. We boys hardly ever got out past the walls to see for ourselves. Once a year, on Fourth of July, the Charity Ladies, who put up money for the Home, took the boys to some lake to see how many of us would drown. At Christmas they'd take us over to the Girls' Home for a party, where the boys didn't do anything but fight and throw food.

That was about it. We didn't have any clear idea of how things were in the outside world. It was a mystery to us. We knew there were such places as stores, where you could buy apples or honey and things if you had some money; but we never had any money, so stores didn't matter much to us. We knew that boys out there had bicycles to ride on, baseball bats, and sleds to slide down steep streets on in the winter, for we read stories about boys doing such things in our reading books. But we didn't know what it felt like to ride a bike or slide down a street on a sled. Anyway, we weren't sure that we could do these things even if we got outside ourselves. Maybe boys who grew up in Homes weren't allowed to have bicycles and sleds. We didn't know.

But Cook had spent most of his life, until the last ten years, outside the Home, and he still went out every Sunday afternoon to visit an old widow woman he was soft on. Cook liked boasting about all the things he'd done other places, and we encouraged him, for we were mighty curious about the outside world. When me and Billy were sent into the kitchen to scrub pots and pans, we always got Cook talking about such things if we could.

We switched off, one washing, one drying. This time, as soon as we got a few pots done so it looked like we were being industrious, Billy said, "Cook, you ever know any rich people out there?" We knew he'd say he had, whether he had or hadn't. We liked hearing about rich people.

Cook was stirring a big pot of beans. "Sure. I knew plenty of them rich. When I was out there in Californy back a while, workin' in this here hotel, them rich men was a dime a dozen."

"How'd they get so rich, Cook?" Billy said. I knew he was trying to figure out some way to get himself rich.

"Diggin' for gold." Cook looked around to see if we believed him. We knew enough to look like we did. "Was layin' around all over the ground out there in them days. I know—I seen it. I seen a whole lake fulla gold once. Up in some mountains." He turned back to stir the beans.

"A lake full of gold?" I said. A lot of things Cook said were hard to believe, but this was harder than most. "Where was the gold, just floating around in the water?"

"Gold doesn't float, you dummy," Billy said.

"You don't know as much as you think you do, Billy," I said. "Maybe there's some kind of gold that floats."

Cook looked around at us. "Neither of you know nothin' about it. I seen it. You didn't." Cook was wearing a dirty undershirt. He was getting stooped from being old and didn't shave but once a week when he visited the widow woman he was soft on.

"Well, then, where was it?" Billy said.

"Bottom," Cook said. "Gold all over the bottom of that there mountain lake. Great big chunks of it. Some of 'em big as your fist."

Well, I wanted to believe it. It was nice to think that there might be some gold out there somewhere I could have just for picking it up. But it wasn't an easy thing to believe. I gave Billy a glance to see what he was thinking. His eyes were wide and shining, and I knew right away there was going to be trouble. He said, "Why didn't you dive down and get some?"

3

"You ain't callin' me a liar are you, Billy? I wouldn't if I was you."

"No, no, Cook," Billy said. "I believe you." If Cook thought you doubted his word he'd clam up on you and then there'd be nothing for entertainment but scrubbing pots. "I wasn't calling you a lair."

"You ain't in any position to call no one a liar, Billy Foster," Cook said. "Keep it in mind."

Cook was right about that. Billy was the blamedest one for lying. He could think up lies faster than most people could talk—mix in some facts here and there to throw you off and give it flavor—and before you were finished, he'd have you believing that snow was cream cheese and pigs could fly. Leastwise he'd have the boys believing it. I don't guess Billy got a whole lot past Deacon and his sister, who ran the Home: not much got by them. But he could put it past the boys. Me, I was different—just not a natural hand for lying the way Billy was. I didn't have a feeling for it, was likely to blurt out the truth before I caught myself. Not Billy. Oh, the boys just admired Billy so for the lies he'd tell to Deacon or his sister or Staff. Where if a boy dropped a plate and broke it, he'd say it was because some other boy jogged his elbow. Not Billy; that wasn't original enough for Billy. Instead he'd say that it was the cat's fault. For when one of the boys started to sing, the cat took fright, leaped for an open window, and when Billy reached out to save it from an awful death, why it was natural that the plate would fly out of his hands and break. Or if

Billy stole a couple of doughnuts off Deacon's breakfast tray, and they happened to slip out from under his shirt while he was carrying the tray up, he'd wheel around and shout, "What blamed boy threw those doughnuts?" even if there wasn't anyone around big enough to throw a doughnut that far. The boys just loved to hear Billy tell stories, for Billy didn't mind what he said to anybody; and if he knew he'd got a good audience of boys listening, he'd roll along until Deacon or somebody stopped him. Of course it didn't ever do him any good. In the end Deacon or Staff or whoever it was would say, "I never heard such a natural-born liar in my life, Billy Foster," and wallop the tar out of him.

So that's what Cook meant when he said that Billy wasn't in any position to call anyone a liar. He said, "I wasn't calling you a liar, Cook. I was just curious is all. Why didn't you dive down and get some of that gold?" Billy was up to something.

Cook calmed down. "Couldn't swim," he said. "Still can't. Never learned how. Durn funny thing, too. I was raised up close enough to a creek so's I could spit into it from the henhouse roof, and fished in it every spare minute I got. Never got the hang of swimmin'. The other kids all swum in that there creek, but the first time I tried it I sunk like a stone and had to be hauled out cryin' and splutterin'. It kinda discouraged me. Never tried it again. Once was enough."

Billy gave Cook a look. "Where was this lake? Out in California?"

"Nope. Over there somewheres past Plunket City. Was workin' on the railroad at the time."

I didn't know where Plunket City was, but I'd heard Staff mention it, so I knew it couldn't be too far off. I figured I'd better get Billy off Plunket City and that lake of gold before he got too hot about it. "I guess somebody's come along and cleaned that gold out of there by now," I said.

"Doubt it," Cook said. He lifted a wooden spoon full of beans from the pot and touched them with his tongue to see if they were getting hot. Beans were the usual supper at the Home. Cornmeal mush for breakfast, bread and molasses for lunch, beans and fatback for supper. Black coffee so bitter you could hardly swallow it. Deacon Smith said we were orphans and didn't deserve any better—no milk for the coffee, no ketchup for the beans, no jam for the bread.

"See, Possum?" Billy said "That gold's still there."

"What makes you think so?" I said.

Cook gave me a look to see if I was calling him a liar this time. Then he said, "Can't nobody find the durn place. Way I heard it, some fella I was workin' with on the railroad in Plunket City told me he brought a chunk a gold big as a baseball outta there. Didn't have it no more. Lost it to another fella in a poker game. There was heaps of it still up there, this fella said. I went on up into them mountains with nothin' but a jackknife, loaf a bread, hunk a cheese. Got myself lost the first day. There's somethin' queer about them mountains. Turn a corner and suddenly you're someplace else and can't find the way back you come. Never seen nothin' like it."

I knew blame well that Billy wanted to run off from the Home and find that gold lake. Boys ran off now and again. You'd suddenly realize that so-and-so wasn't around anymore. But mostly it was older boys—fourteen, fifteen. Me and Billy weren't but twelve, thirteen, depending on when our birthdays were. We'd come to the Home at about the same time. Were babies together in the same crib, slept together in the same bed after that—two to a bed was the rule there. Pretty much did everything together all our lives. Sometimes it seemed like I knew what Billy was going to think before he did.

But Billy knew how old he was, and I didn't. Mostly when a kid was brought to the Home, whoever brought him knew the facts of him—when he was born, who his folks were. Deacon wasn't allowed to say who your folks were. There was some law about it where nobody was supposed to know that you'd given your baby away to a Home. But usually you'd get a name and a birthday out of it, at least.

Not me. They'd found me on the doorstep in a snowstorm curled up in a basket like a possum. No note with me to say when I'd been born, or even if I *had* been born, although I figured I must have been. So far as papers went, I didn't exist. So I didn't have a birthday. But the fact was I *did* have a birthday, for I gave myself one. I knew it had been winter when I'd been left off in the snow, so I gave myself February 22, George Washington's birthday. It worked out pretty good, for George Washington's birthday was a holiday with no school, bands playing, and most people eating pie and cake, leaving aside orphans and such. I could pretend the holiday and the bands were for me, not George Washington, who'd been dead a good while and wouldn't miss it. Of course I didn't tell anyone it was my birthday, for they'd of teased the pants off me. I didn't even tell Billy. I kind of wanted it to be a secret for myself.

So I didn't know exactly how old I really was, but I knew we were too young to run off from the Home. "That's it, then," I said. "You couldn't find that lake if you were paid for it."

Billy didn't pay any attention to that. "Tell us how you found it, Cook."

"Stumbled on it. Wandered around up there two or three days half starved to death, tryin' to find my way down out of there. Lookin' for berries, birds' eggs, anything. I'd of et a live rat. Pushed along till I come to some kind of meadow. Right in the middle of this here meadow was this little lake. Even at that distance I could see it sparkle. Wasn't thinkin' about no gold. Figured there might be fish, frogs, turtles in that lake. Jumped over to it mighty fast, you bet. Water clear as glass. Could see straight down six, seven feet. See everythin' down there plain as day—sand, weeds, and sittin' on the sand among them weeds was chunks of gold. All over the bottom."

Nobody said anything. We were all thinking about the things you could do if you had some gold. I said, "If only you could have swum, Cook."

"I'd have figured out a way to get that gold out of there, even if I couldn't swim," Billy said. "Poke it out with a stick or something."

"How you gonna poke something off the bottom of a lake with a stick?" Cook said. "I was there; you wasn't. Tried every durn thing I could think of. There wasn't no way to do it, less'n you dove down and picked it up with your hands."

The last time the Charity Ladies took us out for the Fourth of July picnic, me and Billy tried to swim. We sank to the bottom just like Cook did.

Billy said, "I'd of tied a rope to a tree so's I could haul myself out with it."

"Where you gettin' that tree from, Billy?" Cook said. "Wasn't one within half a mile. To say nothin' of a rope. Didn't have nothin' but the clothes I was standin' in and my pocketknife. Figured I could maybe scrape a couple of chunks out with a rake if I fixed it up with a long handle. Went down to this little town at the bottom of the mountains they call Wasted Gulch. Got me a rake, a rope, and such."

"I thought you were lost," I said. I figured that'd make Cook sore and he'd stop firing Billy up about that lake.

But it didn't. He just gave me a hard look and went on. "Oh, I was lost, all right. Figured if I kept moving downhill, I had to come out of there sooner or later. Ate berries and turtles and such until I come out. Went on back up there with that rake. Couldn't find the durn lake." He tasted the beans again.

"There must have been some way to find it," Billy said.

"Wouldn't have made no difference. That lake plain disappeared on me."

"That lake disappeared?" Billy said. "How can a lake disappear? A lake can't disappear."

"This one did. Searched all over them mountains for a week and couldn't find it. That there lake disappeared itself."

"Oh, come on, Cook," Billy said.

Cook shook his head. "Don't be such a smart mouth, Billy. You don't know nothin' about it. I was there; you wasn't." He lowered his voice. "It was witchery. It knowed I was comin' back for its gold and it disappeared itself."

Billy laughed. "You're crazy, Cook. A lake can't disappear itself."

"Billy didn't mean that, Cook," I said.

It was too late. Cook snatched the big wooden spoon out of the bean pot and took a swipe at Billy. A half-dozen beans flew through the air.

Then we realized that Deacon Smith was standing at the kitchen door. "Cook," he said in his sharp, high voice. "I don't want these worthless boys standing around like gentlemen of leisure. If you can't keep them busy, I'll find something else for them to do. Once more and somebody's in for a licking."

Cook pulled at the tuft of white hair that stuck up over his forehead. "Yes, sir," he said.

"I thought I said I didn't want these boys working together. One's more worthless than the other."

"They come in together. You can't pry 'em apart."

"Stick a toasting fork in their behinds and you'll pry them apart fast enough. I don't want them together."

By this time we were back at the sink, heads down, scouring out pots and pans as hard and fast as we could. Deacon Smith liked nothing better than a chance to whip a boy with his thin cane. It was pie and ice cream to him.

Chapter Two

The real name for the Home was Deacon Smith Home for Waifs. When the boys were feeling funny, which wasn't too often, they called it Deacon Smith Home for Whipping, for Deacon and his sister took a good deal of pleasure in whipping boys when they could think of the least excuse. Billy came in for his share of it, all right. I usually could see it coming, and I'd warn him.

"I can't help it, Possum. I got to do something bad every once in a while so as to feel comfortable with myself. I get to feeling itchy and scratchy if I don't."

"If it was only once in a while, it mightn't be so bad. It's more like once a week."

"Nah. You're always exaggerating, Possum." The next thing we knew, Deacon's sister would be all over us shouting, "What are you two talking about?" And I'd be in for it along with Billy.

Oh, Deacon, he warned me about Billy often enough. "You stay away from Billy Foster, Possum. He's corrupting you. One day you'll get hanged alongside him." It didn't matter what Deacon said about Billy. Me and Billy had been together near every minute of every day and night since we came to the Home, and we generally found a way to keep together. Considering the way the other boys admired him, it made me proud to be Billy's best friend.

So I knew if I didn't talk Billy out of running off to find that lake of gold, I might have to go with him. We talked about it the next day when Staff set us to hoeing tomatoes and corn in the truck garden back of the barn. "Billy," I said, "you can't believe anything Cook says. He hasn't got any brains at all. He can't even tie his own shoes. He slips out of them at night without untying them so he doesn't have to tie them in the morning. I saw him do it once."

"That's just it, Possum. Cook isn't smart enough to make up a story like that."

"Well, even so," I said, "how come nobody else came along and cleaned that lake out?"

"They couldn't find it," Billy said.

"Billy, for blame's sake, that lake didn't disappear itself."

"I never said it did. Cook couldn't find it the second time. Wasn't smart enough to leave a trail or notice the landmarks. If somebody had cleaned that gold out of there, the story'd be everywhere."

"Billy, we aren't old enough to run off yet."

"Sure we are. Possum, if we got out of here, you could fix yourself up with a birthday."

"I don't mind about that," I said. I didn't say I'd already fixed myself up with a birthday.

"Yes, you do. You could get a last name, too."

That was another problem I had: I had no last name—the only kid in the world who didn't have one, I figured, although I wasn't sure about that. When they saw me curled up in the basket they started calling me Possum. Just put me down on the books like that—*Possum.* By the time I got big enough to understand about last names, it was too late. When I asked Deacon if I couldn't have a last name, he told me I was an orphan and shouldn't be asking for special favors; I should be grateful that somebody was willing to take me in and see that I got an education and fatback and beans regular as clockwork. He forgot to mention that the Charity Ladies gave him a stipend every month for the services he did us boys.

Not having a last name wasn't so bad when it was only the boys, but it was troublesome with anyone else. Somebody like the Charity Ladies, or school inspectors, were always asking for my last name. When I told them I didn't have one, they said it couldn't be, everybody had a last name; and when I said I couldn't help that, I didn't have one, they gave each other funny looks and wrote something down in their notebooks. I figure that what they wrote down wasn't very polite. "Do you really think I could get fixed up with a last name on the outside, Billy?"

"Sure as I'm standing here."

He was bound to answer something like that, but I figured it might be true. "How'd it work?"

"Oh," he said, real easy, like he'd spent half his life getting last names for people. "You go to an office somewhere and pay them a dollar and they fix it up for you. Stamp it on some papers."

"Where'd I get that dollar? I haven't seen anything bigger than a nickel my whole life."

"Why, from the gold, dummy. Once we find that gold we're going to have bushel baskets full of dollars. Just take one out of a basket and give it to the fella in the office. Two minutes later you got a last name."

Well, he didn't know anything more about it than I did, but I figured there was some truth in it. Deacon, he was always going on mighty important about having to go downtown to see about somebody in this office or that office. There was bound to be an office for names. But I didn't get a chance to think more about it right then because Staff came wheeling around the corner of the barn and shouted that if we didn't start those hoes moving, we'd get something we weren't looking for.

Well, I wanted to do it, and I didn't. I didn't know about that lake full of gold; maybe it was there and maybe it wasn't. But getting out of the Home and maybe getting a last name, too, would be worth about anything I could think of it. Besides, it'd be an adventure, especially doing it with Billy.

But running away would be scary. We didn't know what the world outside was like—didn't know if people were all mean like Deacon and his sister or if some of them were nice. I remember once when I was around six or seven, Cook took sick and wasn't up to much. He sent me off to a store with two dollars and a wagon, to get a sack of beans. I tell you, it was a mighty strange feeling to be away from the Home, trundling along with that little wagon behind me. All at once I realized I could do anything I wanted—I could run, sing, sit down in the sun or look at the things in shopwindows I'd never seen before. So I ambled along, taking my time, looking around at things, and singing to myself. To top it off, the storekeeper gave me a piece of hard candy to suck on. I guess it tickled him to see a little fella come in with a wagon like that. He knew I was from the Home, of course, and took pity on me. I never forgot that.

So there were at least some nice people outside. But how many? And how'd we eat; where'd we sleep; how'd we stay dry in a rainstorm, warm in the snow? Cook told us once about some kids he knew who went to sleep in a barn when the temperature was down to zero; when they woke up in the morning they were frozen to death. I could see easy enough that we might soon wish we were back in the Home eating molasses and bread—just longing for it, maybe.

What tipped it was Billy. Once he got outside, he was certain to get into trouble. Wouldn't last a day. Two days at most. Outside, it wouldn't just be a whipping. He could get half beat to death by somebody he stole something from, get arrested, and sent to jail for ten years—even hung if it was bad enough. And I saw where I couldn't let him go out there and get hung. Besides, I was curious to see what it was like on the outside.

But I had to admit that there was more to it than that. Billy was bound and determined he would do it, maybe not right then, but pretty soon—maybe the next time he got a good licking from Deacon and his sister. There was a good chance he'd run off without me. And then where would I be, all alone in the Home without Billy? Oh, I was friendly enough with the other boys, leaving aside teasing me about my name. I'd have friends enough. But me and Billy were more like brothers—twins, you could say. About the same size, too, except that he had dark hair and mine was light. After all those years, I couldn't see myself doing things without Billy, even if it meant trouble. That was it, more than anything.

It took us a while to figure out how to do it. The Home was just a big old brick building three stories high. There was a barn out back, where the Deacon kept the horse and shay. Farther back was the henhouse and pigsty. Thinnest pig there ever was. Pigs were generally fed on kitchen scraps and table leftovers, but at the Home there weren't any table leftovers and the boys stole the kitchen scraps before they got to the pig. There was a truck garden out back, too, where we grew corn and tomatoes and such. Not that we boys ever saw corn or tomatoes. That went upstairs to the Deacon, his sister, and Staff.

There was a brick wall around the whole thing, which was part of the problem, for they kept the front gate locked most of the time. We couldn't climb over the wall during the day for we'd need a ladder for that, and it wasn't likely Deacon would just nod and say good morning if he saw us going by with a ladder.

So we'd have to escape at night. The problem with that was that they locked the building up tight at bedtime—doors, windows, everything. We had a chance to talk about it a couple of days later when we were washing pots and pans—Cook had gone off to the supply room with Deacon's sister to work up the food order. "There's the loft ladder in the barn," Billy said. "I don't think it's nailed there, just leaning against the wall."

"There's broken glass stuck into the top of the wall," I said. We knew that, because you could see the top of the wall from our dormitory room on the second floor.

"We could throw a couple of horse blankets over it," Billy said. "But how are we going to get out of the house at night?"

"Let's think," I said. We stopped washing pots and pans and pretended we were thinking. It didn't do any good.

"Maybe we could talk Cook into leaving the kitchen door unlocked," Billy said.

"He'd tell the first minute he could."

"We could promise to bring him gold."

"He wouldn't believe us. He knows blamed well we wouldn't bring him any gold."

We thought some more. "I got an idea," Billy said. "In the middle of the night, one of us could pretend to be sick. Pretend to be poisoned. And then when they were running around getting medicine or something, the other one could sneak away and unlock the kitchen door."

"They wouldn't believe anyone was poisoned. What could you get poisoned on around here?"

"Some mornings that coffee'd poison a horse," Billy said. "Smells like old cabbage poured out of a boot."

"They wouldn't believe it unless all the boys who drank the coffee was poisoned."

"Well, then, an appendix attack. Holler and hang on to your side like you could hardly bear it." He was almost more excited about the fun of playacting than escaping. "Then the other one leaps out of bed and shouts for Deacon. When they come rushing upstairs, the one that's downstairs is getting the kitchen door open. Then he gets the ladder out of the barn, leans it against the wall, and goes over. By and by the sick one gets better, and when things have calmed down he slips away and goes over the wall, too."

I stood there thinking about it. "I don't know, Billy. There's a lot that could go wrong with it."

"Nah," he said. "Nothing's going to go wrong. It's sure to work. And then we'll be out of the Home. A week later we'll be up there in those mountains by Plunket City scooping gold out of that lake by the bushel."

"You forgot to put in a half hour where we learn how to swim."

"Don't worry about swimming, Possum. I can swim."

"Last time I saw you swimming you were three feet under the water and would have drowned if one of the Charity Ladies hadn't come and hauled you out."

"Nah, I wasn't drowning. Nothing like drowning. Would have been swimming like a champ if I hadn't of choked on some loose water."

I gave him a look, but I didn't say anything. You couldn't talk Billy out of anything he didn't want to be talked out of.

Well, the whole thing was making me plenty scared, all right. If anything went wrong and we got caught, we'd get whipped bloody and put on bread and water for a month. If we got away, there was nineteen

other things to worry about—starving, getting frozen
to death, chewed up by wild dogs, and most likely of
all, getting arrested for something Billy did. That was
about as certain as anything. When you got down to it,
I didn't want to do it. But I saw that we were going to.

Chapter Three

Both of us knew that the one doing the playacting would have to be Billy. I wasn't any good at lying. Every time I tried it I'd start stammering and blushing, and the one I was lying to would say, "Give it a rest, Possum." Oh, I wanted to be a good liar, like Billy, and tried practicing to myself. Practice helped; I got to where I could lie pretty easy when it was to myself, for I already knew I was lying and had got used to it. But when I tried it on somebody else, here came the stammering and blushing, and finally I gave it up.

So it would be Billy who acted sick, and me who would open the kitchen door and lean the ladder against the wall.

We needed a real dark night. We kept watching. Finally a day came when it started clouding over in the middle of the afternoon. By supper time the whole sky was covered with gray, low-hanging clouds, puffy and rolling along at a good clip. We got a chance to talk a little when Cook set us to carrying slops out to the pig. "What are we going to do if it rains?" I said.

"It won't rain," Billy said.

"Well then, what are those gray clouds supposed to be?"

Billy looked up at them. "Maybe it won't rain hard."

But when I thought about it, I saw there was no choice. A dark night meant clouds, and clouds meant the chance of rain. "I guess we can stand getting wet," I said.

We went to bed at nine as usual. Staff paraded around for a while with the dormitory door partly open so he could see that there was a head on every pillow, if you could call the thin sacks of feathers they gave us pillows. Then he went out and shut the door.

Staff didn't care for hanging around the dormitory any more than we cared to have him there. I lay next to Billy. I figured I was too keyed up to go to sleep, but the next thing I knew Billy had hold of my arm and was whispering, "Wake up, Possum. I'm going to start."

"I *was* awake," I whispered back.

"No you weren't. You were snoring."

"Never mind that," I said. "Just start."

For a moment he was silent. Then he oozed out a low moan, sort of an owl sound. "Oooo, oooo." I waited.

"Ooooo," he went again, and then "aaaaw." I had to admire him, for it sounded mighty real. "Aaaaw," he went again, louder this time. Then, "Ooooo."

I decided it was time for me to chime in. "What's the matter, Billy?"

"Sssh," he whispered. "Not yet. I'm just getting to the good part."

Blame if he wasn't having fun. That was Billy—nothing he liked better than putting one over on somebody. For him it was better than ginger cookies.

"Listen to this," he whispered. Suddenly he cried out, "Aaaugh." Then he went back to moaning again. "Oooo, oooh."

I could hear a couple of boys sit up in bed. "Who's that?" somebody said.

Now I had to get into it. "Are you OK, Billy?" I said fairly loud. It didn't sound right to me, but nobody seemed to notice.

"I don't feel so good, Possum. It hurts awful right here."

"Where's that, Billy?" The whole thing was making me blush, and I was glad it was dark in there.

"Right here," Billy said. "Oooo. Right here on my left side. Don't touch it."

"Left side, Billy? Maybe you got an appendix attack."

"What's going on?" a boy said in the dark.

I jumped out of bed, wanting to quit the playacting as soon as I could. "Billy's mighty sick. I think he's having an appendix attack."

24

"Oooo, oooo. Aaaugh."

"I'll get Deacon, Billy," I said nice and loud. Quickly I slid into my clothes. The boys were all pretty much awake by now, and in the dim light coming in under the door I could see their shapes sitting up in the bed. I jumped into my shoes and, without waiting to tie the laces, made for the door. Some of the boys were out of bed now, going over toward Billy to get in on the excitement. In a moment I was in the hall. I hit the stairs and began to shout, "Come quick, come quick, Billy Foster's dying of a appendix attack." I pounded up the stairs to the third floor, where Deacon and his sister lived, making as much noise as I could. "Somebody come quick," I shouted again.

As I hit the top of the stairs, the door to Deacon's rooms swung open and Deacon's sister stuck her head out. She was wearing a nightie covered with pink roses and a nightcap to match. "What's this? What are you doing up at this hour of the night?"

"Billy Foster's real sick, ma'am. His left side hurts so he can hardly touch it."

"Left side?" she said sharply.

"Yes. Right here," I said, pointing to where I figured my appendix was.

"There?" she said, poking at me. Just then the door opened wider and Deacon himself came into view. He was also wearing a nightshirt and nightcap, but without pink roses. "What's all this? he said sternly.

"One of the boys is ill," she said. "Nine times out of ten they're malingering. Waking honest people in the middle of the night just to be annoying. But you'd better have a look."

"If it isn't one thing, it's the next," Deacon said. "Wait till I put on some clothes." He disappeared.

Deacon's sister went on standing there. I was stuck. Blame her, why didn't she go down to tend to Billy? Two boys appeared at the bottom of the stairs. "Is somebody coming, Possum? Billy's took real bad."

"What a nuisance," Deacon's sister said.

"He's thirsty as can be," I said. "I better get him some water from the kitchen."

She gave me a look. "If he's having trouble with his internal organs, he shouldn't drink anything."

"Oh," I said, trying to think of something else.

But she wasn't paying attention to me. "I'd better have a look myself," she said, more to herself than to me. "*He* won't have the faintest notion what to do." She shut the door to get dressed.

I turned and raced down for the kitchen. It was dark in there, but enough of a glow came from the coal stove so I could make my way to the kitchen door. I fumbled around and found the key under the knob. I gave it a twist and felt the lock click. I eased the door open, slipped through, and shut it again. Luckily it wasn't raining yet. For a few seconds I stood there in the dark, feeling my heart thumping away like a drum and taking a couple of deep breaths. Nobody would miss me right away. Not with the boys all milling around the dormitory—wouldn't miss me for a while, not until they made a bed check, which they were bound to do once the excitement died down. Still, there wasn't any time to waste. I trotted toward the barn, moving as quick as I could. It was almighty dark—we'd figured that right at least. I couldn't see anything until it was a foot in front of me and kept stumbling over stones and tree roots. Once I ran smack into the lilac bush by the drive where it came up to the barn, and another time I came near ramming my head into a maple tree but saw it just in time.

Finally I was close enough to the barn to see the door. I heaved on it. It made a heavy, groaning sound as I slid it open a couple of feet. I prayed there was enough noise going on in the dorm to cover the sound. I slipped inside the barn, holding my hands in front of my face, just in case I stepped into a pitchfork or a pickax, and worked my way along to where the ladder went up to the loft.

I started to tip it down sideways, but it was heavier than I figured and it came crashing down and hit the barn floor with a bang. "Blame it," I said aloud. I grabbed ahold of it and started dragging it out of there, grunting and sweating a good deal. I shoved the ladder through the door, and then I felt my way back to the rear of the barn, got a couple of horse blankets off the pile, and carried them outside. I slid the barn door shut and, clutching the blankets under one arm, lifted the ladder with both hands and staggered through the blackness across the yard, stumbling and cursing and sweating.

Finally I saw the outline of the wall in front of me, lit up a little by the thin glow of gas lamps outside somewhere. I dropped the blankets and heaved the ladder until it was upright and leaned it against the wall. I picked up the blankets and put my foot on the bottom rung. Then I heard a sound in the dark, not more than five feet away. I jumped and near dropped the blankets. "Where in blazes are you, Possum?" came a whisper.

"Billy? How'd you get out?"

"Never mind that. Let's go."

I started up the ladder with the horse blankets, climbing as quick as I could. Suddenly the kitchen door crashed open, and there came a shout: "Come back here, boy, or I'll beat you until you scream for mercy," Deacon hollered. "You think you can fool me, but you can't."

I went on up the ladder to the top and dropped the horse blankets over the glass jutting from the top of the wall. I swung my head around to see where Billy was. Back toward the house a hand all by itself was swinging a lantern, making the shadows of the trees race around the yard. With my fist, I banged at the spurs of glass under the blanket, cracking some off under the heavy cloth. In a few seconds, a couple of feet along the top of the wall was flat. "Where are you, boy?" came a cry.

Now Billy was up the ladder right behind me. "Hurry up," he said in a low voice. I slid myself gingerly onto the wall, hoping that a piece of glass wouldn't decide to poke itself into my stomach. Once more I looked back. The lantern was coming closer.

"Jump," Billy said. I hadn't figured on jumping from an eight-foot wall. I'd reckoned we'd pull the ladder up behind us and climb down the other side at our convenience. But there wasn't time for that. I swiveled around, dropped my legs over the side, and grabbing hold of the edge as best I could, let myself dangle. I couldn't see a blamed thing down below me. Praying I wasn't over a ditch or a heap of stones, I let go.

The next thing I knew, I was lying on my back with the wind knocked out of me. "Watch out, Possum," Billy said in a low voice. I rolled over out of the way just as Billy landed with a thump. "Ow," he said.

I jumped to my feet. From behind the wall I heard Deacon shout, "Aha." Then we were running up the street as fast as we ever ran, away from the Home, headed for glory.

Chapter Four

We didn't know where we were or where we were running to; we were just running along in the dim gaslight, down one street, up an alley, out the other, making a turn, going on for a couple of blocks, making another turn, zigzagging away from the Home. It didn't seem real to me. I felt closed in on myself, and whatever was outside me—the cobblestones, the street lamps, the houses flashing by—wasn't real, but was out of a dream. I couldn't remember why I was running; I was just running.

On we went, minute after minute, until we were puffing and blowing so heavy it felt like our lungs were rubbed raw. Finally we couldn't run anymore, and we stopped. We stood on a corner, dripping sweat and sucking in air with big fluttery gasps. "We made it,"

Billy gasped out. His eyes were shining, and he grabbed my hand and shook it. "We made it, Possum. They'll never get us back there now."

But I wasn't so sure we were safe yet. "Sssh. Let's listen." We listened, but we didn't hear any sound of running feet. Still, I was worried. "He's bound to come after us. He doesn't want to lose our stipend. I don't know how much trouble he'll go to get us back, but we best keep on moving, soon as we catch our breath."

"Naw," Billy said. "He's probably put us out of his mind already. They'll never catch us now."

That was Billy. When he got confident like that people would generally go along with him. "Still, we better not take a chance," I said.

Billy turned, and now I noticed that his face was pretty well scratched up. "Where'd you get all those scratches from, Billy?"

"I'll tell you," he said. "Let's go." We set off again, this time trotting along a little more reasonable. We had no idea where we were, but it didn't much matter, so long as we made sure to keep the Home behind us. As we went, Billy told me the story.

"Well, Deacon, he came storming up, tucking in his shirt and shouting to the boys to cut the hollering and go back to their beds or he'd beat them all within an inch of their lives. But they were too heated up to stop clamoring around, for they figured I was going to die, and they wanted to stay close enough so they wouldn't miss it. A couple of the little ones were cry-

31

ing, but they still wanted to watch. I just lay there, moaning and groaning and trying to work up a decent sweat, and here came Deacon. He set himself down on the edge of the bed and said, 'Where does it hurt, Billy?' I showed him. He kind of took a poke at it with his finger, like he was testing a cake to see if it was done. I let out a holler that near took his head off. The little kids began to wail and the big ones let out a whoop, like they could see the end was near. To keep the clamor going long enough so's you could get that ladder out of there, I shouted, 'Look out, Deacon, I got to throw up.' He leaped off the bed like he was stuck with a knife and yelled, 'Open the window, one of you little fools.' Some kid raced over and opened the window, and I staggered over to it, kind of coughing and gasping.

"I hit the window and looked out. Down below was that lilac bush that reaches near up to the windowsill. I made a noise like I was about to throw up. Then I pulled back in a little ways and had a quick look. Deacon had his back to me, heading out. I reckoned he was going to fetch his sister. So I put my head out the window again, leaned way out, put my arms across my face, and slid out into that lilac bush."

"You slid out of the second floor? You might of killed yourself."

"I reckon I blame near did. I started crashing down through that lilac like a sack of meal. So I let go of my face and started grabbing at the bush. That slowed me down some, but that's when I got scratched up. How bad does it look?"

"I don't expect you'll die from it, but you ought to clean yourself up before you frighten somebody," I said.

"I figure that lilac came out of it worse than I did. I must of smashed it all to smithereens. I kind of lay there on the ground in sort of a daze. I could hear the kids up there shouting, 'Billy died and fell out the window, Billy died and fell out the window.' They were mighty disappointed they didn't see me pass away."

"You really slid out the window, Billy?"

"I swear it, Possum. I saw my chance, and I took it." He pulled the tail of his shirt out, wiped off his face, and looked at the shirt under a streetlight. "It doesn't look like I'm bleeding anymore."

That was Billy. I had to admire him. He'd take a chance on anything. But still, I knew I better keep a watch on him.

We were coming into a more cheerful place. There were some restaurants here, saloons, a couple of theaters, some three-story brick houses. It must have been three, four o'clock at night, as close as I could figure, but a lot of the saloons were still open. We'd never been anywhere near a saloon before, but we'd heard about them from reading Cook's *Graphic*—which his widow woman gave to him each week. Haunts of the Devil, the *Graphic* said they were. We were curious, and we stopped to look in one.

It looked kind of nice in there—not what you'd call homey, but cheerful. A couple of men were leaning up against the bar chatting, another one was asleep with his head down on a table, two women in short skirts and long stockings were at another table drinking beer, and an old guy sat at the piano, smoking a cigar, but not playing anything. It was near to daytime and pretty quiet.

"I wish we had some money so we could go in there," Billy said.

"Me, too. Although maybe we ought to keep moving. Maybe Deacon's got the cops out after us now."

"I want to look for just another minute," Billy said. "I wonder what those girls are all dressed up for."

"I think they must have been in a show." I'd never seen a show, but I'd read about shows in the *Graphic*. "I wonder what kind of show it was."

But before we could talk about it, one of the men at the bar raised up his beer mug, swallowed off the last of it, slapped the other men on the back, and came marching out. He was wearing a big black hat with a wide brim, an old blue jacket with a button missing, and dark brown boots, pretty worn but polished up good. He came swaggering out toward us, and we stepped back to let him come through the door. Then, just as he was in front of us, Billy grabbed at his jacket sleeve. "'Scuse me, sir, but we're hungry as can be and haven't got any money."

The man stopped and looked us up and down. "What're two kids like you doing out on the town at four o'clock in the morning? Where do you belong?"

I wished Billy hadn't done it. It made me nervous. I could see where we needed money, but I figured we oughtn't to be attracting attention to ourselves just yet.

But there was no stopping Billy. "Sir, Pa died last year and Ma's too sick and can't get out of bed. We're awful hungry."

He stood looking at us for a moment. "Pa's dead and Ma's sick, eh? Better get yourself a new story, son—that one was wore out when Washington was president. Everybody's sick to death of it. Now, if you told me your pa was in jail and your ma was too drunk to get out of bed, I might have bought it, although that one's pretty frayed around the edges, too. No, you got to get yourself a story with a little more interest to it. Like you came in from your pa's farm to sell the pig, only the pig got away from you and you don't dare go home until you raise the price of a pig. Something along those lines."

"All right," Billy said. "What if I said I was an orphan from Deacon Smith's Home and escaped by pretending to be dying and slid out of a second-story window into a lilac bush?"

The man laughed. "That's stretching it some, but it's better." He slapped Billy on the shoulder. "What about your pal—he slide out of a window, too?"

35

"Naw, Possum wouldn't do that. He's not as wild as me. He slipped out when I pretended to be dying and slung a ladder up against the wall. We escaped over the ladder. Deacon came near to catching us. He wasn't but twenty feet behind us when we jumped off the wall."

"Where'd you get all them scratches?" the man said.

"I told you," Billy said. "I slid out of a window into a lilac bush."

"Got in a fight, that's clear enough."

"How much you gonna give us?" Billy said.

"How about a nickel apiece."

"Not enough," Billy said. "How 'bout a dime?"

The man laughed. "Oh, all right," he said. He took out of his trousers pocket a small purse held closed with a drawstring, pulled it open, took out two dimes, closed the purse, and slipped it back into his trousers pocket. "Here," he said. "But you better think of something more believable than sliding into a lilac bush. That's pushing it too hard." Then he turned and crossed the street, whistling "Little Brown Jug" to himself.

"He had a lot of money in that purse," Billy said. "Do you reckon he's a gambler?"

"I hope we don't have to beg," I said. "I don't want to do that. We'll only attract attention to ourselves. We got to find jobs."

Billy wasn't listening. "I think we ought to follow that fella."

"What for?" I said.

"Just to see where he goes. He's got a lot of money."

I gave Billy a look. "Now, Billy. No steal—"

"I didn't say I was going to steal anything, did I?"

"You didn't say it, but that's what you were thinking."

"No I wasn't," Billy said. "I wasn't thinking about stealing at all. Maybe he'll give us a job."

"Billy," I said. "I've known you too long. I'll go along with stealing if we're starving to death and can't come up with anything else. But you got to promise we won't steal anything until I agree to it."

He looked at me, kind of wrinkling up his brow, which made the scratches on his face wriggle. "I never could figure out what you got against stealing, Possum."

"Going to jail is what I've got against stealing. What's the point of escaping from the Home if we end up in jail?"

"We won't go to jail," Billy said.

"All the same, you got to promise."

He looked down and then up and away. "All right," he said finally.

"You promise?"

"Blame it, Possum, what's wrong with stealing?"

"You got to promise."

He looked down again. "Oh, all right. I promise. But I'm not going to stand around starving to death if there's a dollar bill sticking out of somebody's pocket."

"We won't starve to death," I said.

"How do you know? Maybe we will."

"How do you know we won't go to jail?"

He couldn't answer that one, so he said, "Well, anyway, I think we ought to follow that fella. Maybe he knows of someplace we can buy some food with our dimes. I could eat a horse."

That made sense. He seemed like a friendly fella. "OK," I said. "Maybe he knows where we can get a job sweeping out a stable or something."

The sky was beginning to lighten a bit—at least the darkness was getting thinner—and we could see the man ambling along toward the end of the block. He turned the corner and disappeared. We trotted after him. At the corner we stopped and looked around.

He was standing beside a little wagon with a sort of house built onto it. A *van*, you might call it. There was a door in the back with a step below, a window with geraniums in a box under it in the side, and probably the same on the side we couldn't see. I knew they were geraniums, because Deacon's sister raised them, and I'd watered them often enough.

Now the fella opened the door, took off his hat, and tossed it through the door. Next he tossed his jacket in. Then he sat down on the step, pulled off his boots, and threw them one by one in over his shoulder. Finally he pulled off his trousers and, wearing his underwear and shirt, climbed into the van and shut the door.

"What's he doing undressing in the middle of the street?" Billy said.

"Probably not much room inside," I said.

"Come on; let's go see."

I didn't trust Billy—he was up to something. But I was mighty curious about that van. I never saw anything like it before. Never even heard of one—they never had anything about it in the *Graphic*. Probably the fella was already asleep, considering what time it was. Maybe in the morning he'd give us a job, and we could travel around with him in the van.

So we slipped along the street until we came up behind it. Billy put his ear against the door. "He's snoring to beat the band," he whispered. "I wonder where the horse for it is?"

"In a stable somewheres, I reckon," I said. "I wonder what it looks like inside."

"Let's peek in."

I knew we shouldn't, but I was blame curious. "Let's not get caught." We went around to the side, and I stood up on my tiptoes. But the window was blocked with a curtain. I slipped around to the front of the van. There was a seat hitched to the house, where the driver sat, but no window there. I went to the other side and stood on tiptoe again.

This time I could see in. The sky had got lighter, and I could see that fella laying face-up on a little cot, his mouth wide open, snoring. It was easy to see why he'd got undressed in the street, for the place was

39

packed with boxes, suitcases, crates, and sacks. He was in some kind of business, that was clear. He wasn't much of a hand for neatness, though.

I was trying to get a look at the boxes and crates to see what was in them, when the rear door started to ease open all by itself, an inch at a time. For a minute I stood there frozen, and then I realized it was that blame Billy. His promise hadn't lasted ten minutes.

The door was now open a good six inches. A hand suddenly appeared and began moving from side to side like the head of a snake. Then it found what it was looking for—that fella's pants. What was I ever going to do with Billy?

I jumped away from the window, and, moving as quiet as I could, slipped toward the back of the van. But I had hardly taken three steps when there came a shout from inside the van: "I gotcha, kid."

Chapter Five

My heart began to thump so loud I could hear it, and I came near to running away and leaving Billy to get out of it the best way he could. I could see the fella kneeling at the door amongst the boxes and crates. He'd got his hand clamped around Billy's hand. Billy's hand was clenched around the pants, so he couldn't let them go. "I figured it," the fella said, taking a quick look at me as I came around the corner. "I knew you kids was bound to be up to something. I didn't have no intention of going to sleep."

"I wasn't trying to steal," Billy said.

"You wasn't trying to steal?" the fella roared, shaking Billy's hand so hard the pants flapped. "Are you trying to tell me your hand slipped into my van all by itself, without you knowing anything about it?"

"I made a mistake," Billy said. "I didn't mean to pick up those pants. I was just feeling around to see if there was a place in here we could sleep. I didn't touch those pants until you squeezed my hand around them."

"Ha, ha," the fella said. "Don't make me laugh; my side hurts."

He looked at me. "And I suppose you was looking in the window by mistake, too."

"Don't blame me," I said. "I told him not to steal."

"Sure," he said. "And the sun don't come up in the morning unlessen the president says it may." He raised up, stepped out of the van, and swung Billy around so he was sitting on the little step. He jerked his head in my direction. "You come over here and sit beside your pal, where I can keep an eye on both of you at once."

I still had a chance to run, and it would have served Billy right if I did. But I didn't; instead I marched over and sat down on the little step next to him. The fella yanked the pants away from Billy and began climbing into them, keeping himself where he could grab ahold of at least one us if we started to make a break for it.

"Blame you, Billy," I said in a low voice. "You promised."

"I couldn't help myself, Possum. Sometimes I just got to do something wrong."

"I would of thought running away from the Home was enough to hold you for a while."

"I'd of thought that, too," he said. "But it wasn't. This feeling just came over me, and I had to go after that purse."

By now the fella had put his pants on and was buckling his belt. "Now then," he said. "Who are you, and what're you doing wandering around town at five o'clock in the morning? And don't give me any song and dance about sliding down a lilac bush."

I looked at Billy and he looked at me. We both knew I'd have to talk us out of it, for Billy'd told too many lies. I looked back at the fella. "What he told you was true. He's always doing things like that. He's kind of wild. We grew up together. He's been like that since he was little."

The fella scratched his head. "Maybe I should take you back to this here orphan home and see if they recognize you."

"No, no," I said, mighty scared. "Please don't. Deacon Smith'll beat the tar out of us and put us on bread and water for a month."

He squinted at me. "You mean this here orphan home is real?"

"I swear to it. We've been there all our lives. We decided we couldn't stand it anymore and escaped. Billy wasn't supposed to slide out the window like that. He saw his chance, and he took it."

"Billy," he said. "You got a last name?"

"Foster. Leastwise, that's what the Deacon's got on the books."

He looked at me. "What's your name?"

I knew what was coming. It always happened with new people, and I hated it. "Possum."

"That's your real name?"

"Yes, sir."

"Possum what?"

"Just Possum. That's all the name they ever gave me." I wished he'd drop it.

"You got to have a last name, Possum," the fella said. "Everybody has one."

Why wouldn't he drop it? I was starting to get stubborn. "Maybe Possum isn't my first name. Maybe it's my last name."

He thought about it for a minute, and then he shook his head. "Nope. Possum's more of a first name. It don't sound like a last name. Look at it this way: which sounds better, Possum McGillicudy or Herbert Possum?"

Neither of them sounded any good to me. I went on feeling stubborn. "I made up my mind. Possum's my last name. I don't care how it sounds."

"Now you don't have a first name anymore," the fella said.

"Maybe it's my first name, too."

"Possum Possum. Who's gonna believe that?"

"Why wouldn't they?"

The fella laughed. "OK, Possum Possum. If that's the way you want it."

Well, it wasn't the way I wanted it. "I didn't say I wanted it for a last name. I only said it might be."

He shrugged. "Have it any way you want. It's no skin off my nose."

I yawned. It was almost daylight, and we hadn't had much sleep. I wasn't feeling so nervous as before, for the fella didn't seem about to take us to the cops. But I was mighty hungry.

Now the fella rubbed his hands together. "Let's say I buy this here story about falling out of a window into a lilac bush. What sort of plans do you fellas have? Aside from stealing my purse. What did you aim to do with yourself once you got of that there home?"

Me and Billy looked at each other. He was a suspicious kind of fella, that was clear, and I wasn't about to say anything about a lake full of gold. "We need to get a job."

"So long as it isn't washing pots and pans," Billy said. "Or anything hard. We don't want to do anything too hard."

"To be honest," I said, "we'd just as soon be moving on. We oughtn't to be setting here like a couple of birds in the wilderness, with Deacon liable to come around the corner any minute."

"Yes, that figures," the fella said. He put his hands behind his back and began to whistle "The Bicycle Built for Two." After a couple of minutes he stopped whistling. "I'll tell you what. The truth is I got a use for a couple of boys with a little larceny in their souls. I don't deny it, I put my hand in somebody else's pocket a time or two. I was particular fond of hoisting gold watches. You could get twenty- five dollars for a good one. There was a trick to it, though, for they was usually hitched on to the fella by a watch chain. The watch is in the vest, most usually, with the chain going through a button hole, or some such. You bumped into the fella like it was an accident, cut the watch chain with a little pair of wire cutters, and hoisted the watch out, all in one motion. Sort of like dealing from the bottom in a poker game—you got to have quick hands. But I gave that all up."

"Why?" Billy said. The whole thing had caught his interest. "I bet I could learn how to do it."

"Don't bother," he said. "Too risky. I got caught once and come close to going to jail. They gave me a lawyer, and he bought the watch off the jail keeper. They said it had got stole. There wasn't any evidence anymore, and I got off. Of course the lawyer kept the watch, said he was entitled to it, for his trouble." He rubbed his hands together again. "No, that game's too risky. I got one now that's safe as churches. But I could use a couple of boys who know how to look sharp and keep their mouths closed."

I didn't exactly like the idea. Whatever his game was, it was certain to be risky. Still, we needed jobs and couldn't afford to be fussy. The best thing was to find out more about it. "How come you don't have a helper now?"

"I did. He ran off last week with forty dollars and my best pair of boots. I should of knew better than to take on somebody who could wear my boots. I want somebody who wears a different size."

"That's us, all right," Billy said. "Me and Possum are just what you want."

"No more sliding down lilac bushes, though, Billy. You got to do just what I say."

"How much do we get paid?" I said.

"Oh that," the fella said. "Let's say we split the take three ways."

I didn't trust that for a minute. "You mean you'd give each of us the same as you'd take for yourself?"

"No. Where'd I say that? I said we'd split it three ways; I didn't say the shares was to be equal. A dollar a day for you each and eats."

To somebody who'd never had more than a nickel at once, a dollar sounded fine. "I don't know where we'd sleep," I said. "There isn't much room in the van."

"Underneath it. I got a square of canvas to lay on and a horse blanket to throw on top of yourself."

"That'll be pretty cold in the winter," I said.

"You won't be around by winter. You'll run off before then—soon as you find something worth running off with."

I didn't like him saying that. He didn't know any-thing about me. "How do you know we'd do that?"

He laughed. "If you was the kind of person who wouldn't run off with valuable goods, you wouldn't of hired on with me in the first place." He rubbed his hands once more. "OK. Let's go get the mules out of the stable and get moving before this here Deacon What's-his-name comes sailing around the corner."

47

Chapter Six

The van was pulled by two mules. We got them out of the stable where he'd been keeping them. We helped him hitch them up, as good as we knew how, and set off through the town. The fella sat up on the driver's seat, flicking a whip at the mules from time to time to remind them of their business, and we trotted alongside to spare the mules, for in town we couldn't make much time, anyway. The mules were dark brown and ornery. They kept looking at me and Billy like they wished we hadn't come along. Billy said under his breath, "Soon as I get a chance I'm going to kick 'em both in the slats."

"You better watch yourself, Billy," I told him. "They can kick a blame sight harder than you can."

But to tell the truth, tired as I was and hungry enough to eat mud, I felt good. We'd done it. We'd run off from the Home a whole lot younger than most boys did. And we'd got some kind of a job already. Of course it was Billy's kind of job, not my kind of a job. I'd try to get Billy to branch off from this fella and go for the lake when I could. I'd just have to see how it went.

But we were free. Free. I could hardly believe it. No more bread and molasses. We could eat pie and ice cream all day if we had the money for it. Blame if that wasn't the nicest part of it all.

We went along for a couple of hours, with the sun rising higher and higher in the sky. Me and Billy were feeling mighty hot, tired, and hungry, but we didn't complain, even though we each knew what the other was feeling and ought to have complained. For every step we took put us farther away from Deacon Smith. I wondered, would he put up posters with our pictures on it, saying RUNAWAY BOYS: $10 REWARD? I reckoned he wasn't likely to go more than ten dollars. Although where he'd get pictures of us I didn't know. Maybe his sister would draw them. She was artistic and always puttering around with a paint box, painting pictures of vases full of flowers, usually, that looked like the vase was on fire. It would be kind of interesting to get your picture painted, but not for a reward poster.

By about ten o'clock the houses were thinning out. The paved street ended, and pretty soon we were going along a dirt road between fields of corn, which at that time of year was up about a foot. Ahead there was a patch of woods. We came up to it. The fella pulled the mules off the road into the shade of the trees and climbed down. He stretched and yawned. "I guess Deacon What's-his-name won't bother us out here. It's time for breakfast."

"That'll suit me," Billy said. "I'm starved." The fella climbed into the back of the van and in a minute came out with a jug of cider, a half-loaf of bread, a chunk of cheese, a jar of mustard, and a piece of ham, all wrapped up in oilcloth. "Here we are, boys, a veritable feast."

"What's a *veritable* mean?" Billy said.

"It don't mean anything. It goes along with *feast.* That's the only kind of feast I ever heard of—*veritable* feast. It's like *fatal error.* If it's an *error*, it's got to be *fatal.* Stands to reason, don't it? Or *treasure trove.* Did you ever hear of a plain *trove?* No, you didn't. That's because there ain't any such thing."

"How can it be a word if there isn't any such thing?" I said.

"All right, Mr. Smarty-pants, what's a trove?"

"Well, I don't exactly know, but it's got to mean something."

"No, it don't. A whole lot of words don't mean anything. Like what I said before, *veritable.* It don't mean anything by itself. It's just meant to hang on to the front of *feast*, to bolster it up. If I told you this here bread and cheese and jar of mustard was a feast, you'd look at me squint-eyed. But if I say it's a *veritable* feast, you'll believe it. That's the thing in my business—making things believable."

I didn't want to argue about it anymore, for I was dead hungry and wanted to use my mouth for other purposes. So we sat down on the ground. The fella took out a good-sized barlow knife; whacked off slices of bread, cheese, and ham; and while me and Billy sat there ramming the food home, he told us about the business.

His name, he said, was Professor Alberto Santini. "Of course that ain't my real name—it ain't nowhere so fancy as that. You don't need to know my real name. No reason to spread it around. The wrong people might remember it. You boys can call me Professor, so we all keep in mind who's top dog around here." He took a swallow of cider.

"Now up ahead here is a little one-horse town called Sabbath. Been through it now and then, but never gave it the benefit of my ministrations. Slim pickings, most likely, but it'll do to break you boys in. First thing we got to do is have a look around and see what sort of business might go. Maybe there's been a epidemic of whooping cough or measles. If that's the case, we go into business with Dr. Cornflower's Purgative Compound, a secret formula of roots and berries that was tortured out of a Nipmuck Indian medicine man. Or maybe you notice that the weather's been dry and the flowers in the yards and window boxes is a little faded and lifeless. In that case we sell 'em Growmore Elixir, scientific miracle imported direct from Gotinbad Laboratories in Germany, where they got peonies ten feet high and rosebushes taller than a house. Or let's say the cattle round about has all got the bloat from eating sour apples. This time we'll bottle up Uncle Fred's Mixture Sixteen, a blend of sixteen different sea salts and minerals passed down for six generations in our family—you boys get to be my nephews for this one—which I got from my old daddy's lips with his last breath. See how it works?" he said, looking from one of us to the other.

Like I figured, it was a skin game. Mighty risky, all right. But I couldn't say that, so to be polite I said, "I guess that's why you got to carry so many different kinds of ingredients in the van."

He laughed. "What ingredients? You wouldn't want to put actual ingredients in these here compounds. Why, you might hurt someone that way. No, it's much the best to stick with water and vegetable coloring, and maybe just a little gunpowder or molasses to liven up the taste. That's where the artistry comes in. You take Dr. Cornflower's Purgative Compound. People don't think nothing of a medicine if it don't taste bad. If it swallers down easy, they figure it can't do them no good. So for the Purgative Compound we aim for a dark brown color and heave in a little shoe polish to give it a real ugly taste."

"Shoe polish?" I said. "Mightn't that poison you?"

"Shoe polish?" the Professor said. "Why, lord no, Possum. A little shoe polish never harmed anyone. Ever see a sick shoe-shine boy? All healthy as horses."

"Maybe you wouldn't see sick ones because they stayed home."

But before the professor could explain that, Billy said, "What about the stuff for the cattle bloat?" He was mighty interested in the whole thing and was following it close.

"Well, there you got something that people ain't likely to taste themselves. Some will, some of these here old farmers are so cheap they'll use cow medicine on themselves when they feel poorly. They figure if it'll fix a cow, it'll fix a human being. But most of 'em got enough sense to see that there's a difference between cows and human beings and will save it for the cows. What you got to do here is make sure there's a powerful smell to the stuff, something that'll knock you down when you open the bottle. Onion salts mixed into kerosene'll do it."

"Pure kerosene?" I said. The whole thing was beginning to worry me. "I know for sure kerosene'll kill you."

"No, no, you got to have some sense about it. You don't want them cows' stomachs catching on fire. You got to put in four or five times as much water. Besides, kerosene costs money. You don't want to eat into the profits by putting in stuff that costs. Use as much water as possible."

Billy was really caught up in it—his eyes were shining. "What about the flower stuff?"

"That should be pretty much all water. It don't do to kill flowers, not until you get out of town, anyway. We sell 'em a bottle of sugar pills with the writing rubbed off. Tell 'em to put one in a gallon of water and pour a quart of the stuff on each flower box every day. You water flowers regular like that, especially during a dry spell, they'll perk right up. Why, it's an act of kindness to these here housewives to take their money, if you look at it that way."

Billy rubbed his hands together and laughed. "It's a humdinger," he said. "Did you think it all up?"

"No, no," Professor Santini said. "I learned at the feet of a master. Dr. Helmut Wolfgang, formerly professor of medical philosophy at the famous Wurtzburger Institute in Darmstadt. A great, great man." He put his hands behind his head, leaned back against a wheel of the van, and gazed up at the sky, like so much greatness was too much for him. "Of course he was from Allentown, Pennsylvania. Ray Cranberry was his real name. But when he swung into that accent, you'd never of guessed that in a million years. He had a spiel that could make a divorce lawyer break down and sob."

"What was his line?" Billy said.

"He had four or five things he could use, depending on how the land lay. His specialty was his Royal Wurtzburger Tonic. All-purpose thing, good for what ails you. Everybody feels low a good deal of the time, so an all-purpose tonic is likely to be a hit, for it takes in near everybody. But it wasn't his line that counted, it was his spiel. When he got warmed up and was going good, people didn't care what he was selling. They wanted to throw money at him. He'd of died a rich man if it wasn't for his weakness."

"What was that?" I asked.

"Feeling sorry for people in trouble. His spiel was so powerful, he got to where he believed it himself. He started giving the tonic away to the needy and went broke." The Professor shook his head. "You always got to fight off the temptation to do good." He clapped his hands together. "Well, time's a wasting. The first thing we need is a reliable source of water." He sent us off into the woods to find a stream or a pond and fill up a couple of five-gallon cans. Then he set off for the little town of Sabbath. We found a stream, filled the cans, and came back and lay in the grass by the van, listening to the mules graze. I was feeling about as content as I ever felt in my life. I had a full belly and no pots and pans to scrub, for the only dish we'd used was the Professor's barlow knife, and he'd wiped it off with a clump of grass.

But there was something bothersome about it. This Professor made Billy look like small change when it came to lying and stealing. He was going to encourage Billy in exactly the wrong direction I wanted him to go. Billy was going to fit in with the whole thing like he was born to it. I leaned up on my elbow to look at him. He'd got a handkerchief over his eyes to keep the sun out and was getting ready to doze off.

"Billy, I want you to keep it in mind that we ran off from the Home to find that gold lake, not traipse around the countryside skinning people."

He didn't move anything but his mouth. "I knew you were going to start up with that, Possum. I just didn't think it'd come so soon."

"Well, just keep it in mind. We didn't run off to skin people. I never agreed to that."

He still didn't move anything but his mouth. "What's wrong with skinning people? It's their own fault."

"Why's it their own fault?"

He took the handkerchief off his eyes and sat up. "Blame you, Possum, what'd you have to bring this up for? I was feeling comfortable as could be and starting to doze off."

I lay back down. "Well, I know," I said. "I'm feeling mighty comfortable myself. But you got to keep in mind what I said. I never agreed to skinning people." He let out a phony snore so as to make his opinion of the matter clear, and we dozed off.

We woke up when the Professor came back from town. "I'm glad to see you two was alert and guarding the van from crooks."

"We weren't asleep," Billy said. "We were just resting our eyes from the sun."

"That's why I didn't hardly have to raise my voice above a roar to get you to open them up," he said.

"We couldn't help it," I said. "Anyone would of fallen asleep after what we did last night."

"Keep it in mind next time."

"What was the town like?" Billy said.

The Professor frowned. "I asked around. Bad luck. There hasn't been any considerable sickness for a spell, and the livestock is all healthy. You can usually count on finding trouble of some kind anyplace you go, but I couldn't turn up any in Sabbath. It's mighty provoking to find people without troubles."

"Maybe we could make them sick some way," Billy said. "I reckon if you mixed up a good dose of kerosene, shoe polish, and onion salts, you'd make them sick pretty quick."

"Yes, that's the right idea, Billy—poison them. But how're you going to get them to swaller enough of it down?"

I hoped they weren't going to try that, for I didn't see how I could go along with poisoning people. Luckily, the Professor decided against it. "Trouble is, if someone died they might get suspicious. No, I'll have to think of something else." He began to whistle "The Old Oaken Bucket" and went off into the van. We could hear him rummaging around in there, and after a bit he came out carrying a small packet. "Here's something that might do." He opened the packet and took out a stack of small labels. Printed on them was a picture of a dog and the words *Thurman's All-Purpose Elixir Formula for Diseases of the Internal Organs*. "You see, boys. It covers most everything but a busted leg or itchy scalp."

"What's the dog for?" I said.

"They were meant for dog medicine. The fella that ordered them never came to pick them up, and I took them off the printer's hands for fifty cents."

"Won't they get suspicious when they see the dog?" Billy said.

"We'll explain that the elixir makes you healthy as a dog. That's a familiar saying—healthy as a dog."

"I never heard it before," I said.

"Well you have now," the Professor said. "After I spiel on it awhile, it'll be familiar enough, around Sabbath, leastwise. All right, where's them water cans?"

We dragged them out in front of the van, and he set to work mixing the elixir, adding a little kerosene here, a little mustard powder there, a dose of red pepper, a dollop of gunpowder, dipping his finger in now and again to taste it. Finally he was satisfied. "There. Take a taste of that, boys. You never tasted anything like it in your lives."

Billy dunked his finger in and sucked it off. "Wow," he said, and spit. "Phew. It tastes like something died in there."

"I told you it was remarkable stuff."

I dipped my finger in but was more cautious and just gave the finger a little lick. It was awful stuff, all right.

"Professor, I don't think anyone could choke down more than a spoonful of that stuff without heaving."

He squinted and took a little taste himself. "Hmmm. Maybe you're right, Possum. That's my problem. I got an artistic nature and can't rest on a thing until I pushed it to the limit. I guess I better toss in a couple more quarts of water." He shook his head, kind of rueful. "Hate to dilute it, though, when I got it so near to perfection."

We spent a couple of hours filling little jars with the elixir and pasting the labels on the jars. Then the Professor spruced us up as good as he could—made us wash our faces and hands in the stream, tuck in our shirts, smooth out our hair with our fingers—and gave us a stack of handbills. They said:

NOTED PROFESSOR ALBERTO SANTINI, SAVANT OF THE HEALING ARTS FINAL TOUR BEFORE DEPARTURE FOR THE COURTS OF EUROPE WHERE HIS MEDICAL WIZARDRY HAS SAVED THE LIVES OF PRINCES

At the bottom he'd inked in, "2 PM, COURTHOUSE SQUARE, ONE APPEARANCE ONLY."

"Get out of town fast; that's the general idea," he explained. "All right, go on into town and stick 'em up everywhere." He gave us a paste pot and a brush, and we went into town.

He was right about it being a one-horse town. There was nothing to it but the main street with the usual shops—butcher, notions, grain-and-feed store with three farmers sitting on the loading platform chewing straw—a couple of churches that needed paint; and down at the end of the street, Courthouse Square. Except there wasn't any courthouse there, just an empty lot with a couple of cows grazing in it.

There weren't hardly any human beings around, either—three or four people ambling along the wooden sidewalk, a couple of shopkeepers standing in their doorways with their arms folded. They were outnumbered by the dogs snoozing in the dusty street.

We began sticking up the handbills where we could. I wondered if someone would try to stop us, but the only person who paid us any attention was the barber standing in the door of the barbershop. As we came by, he stepped out in front of us. "Lemme see one of them," he said. Billy gave him a handbill. "What's this here about? I can't read too good without my glasses."

"Professor Alberto Santini," Billy said. "He's a genius. He cured the king of France of the plague in fifteen minutes. All the doctors over there in France couldn't touch it, no matter what they tried."

The barber squinted at Billy. "I thought they didn't have a king in France no more. I thought they cut off his head awhile back."

"That's right," Billy said. "This was before, when he still had his head on. The Professor waltzed in there, had him stick out his tongue, roll his eyes back, and such. 'It's a real hard case,' he told everybody that was standing around. 'But I got just the thing for it. Thurman's All-Purpose Elixir.' He gave the king a shot of it, and about fifteen minutes later he was getting dressed up to go to a dance."

I stood there with my mouth falling open and my eyes wide. I knew Billy. He wasn't dumb, and he was generally pretty quick to come up with a story when he had to. But I'd never heard him pull anything as smart as this. Of course he'd got the idea of putting in a king from the handbill, where it said the Professor was headed for the courts of Europe. Still, it was pretty smart; I had to admire him for it.

"Keep the handbill," Billy said. "If you know of anybody who's suffering, tell them they'd be a fool to miss out on a chance like this."

I decided to cut in before Billy carried it too far. "Is that really Courthouse Square down there?" I said, pointing. "We didn't see any courthouse."

"There ain't any," the barber said, and spit. "There ain't any library on Library Lane, nor any railroad on Railroad Street. That was just to fool folks when the speculators set the town up back thirty years ago. There was going to be a courthouse, library, grand hotel. You'd of thought they was moving the state capital out here." Then he looked us over. "I don't suppose either of you fellas wants a shave. I'll do it for ten cents each, seeing as you ain't got anything to shave."

But even at ten cents it was more than we could afford. So we said we had to get the handbills up and would maybe come back later. We walked off down the street, and when we were out of the barber's hearing I said, "Billy, I got to hand it to you. I never heard anything so smart. Where'd you get all that stuff?"

He grinned. "It was pretty good, wasn't it? It just came out. I guess I got a knack for this business. Here I've been telling lies all my life for nothing, just giving 'em away. Now I'm going to get paid for 'em. I'm rising up from amateur to professional, you might say."

He was mighty proud of himself, and it got me to thinking. Back there in the Home there wasn't any right or wrong to anything. It was them against us. If you gave it any thought, which nobody did, you'd have a hard time figuring out who was in the wrong. But I was beginning to wonder if it might be different out here. Maybe there was a right and wrong to it now. There wasn't much point in talking it over with Billy, though, so I said, "Billy, you ought to drop the king of France out of it. They cut off his head a long time ago. The Professor couldn't of saved him, unless he was way over a hundred now."

Billy frowned. "Well, all right. Next time I'll make it the king of England."

"They don't have a king, either. They got a queen."

"Blame you, Possum, you're taking all the fun out of it. Who's going to know if they got a king or a queen?"

"A lot of people, I reckon. You'd best make it the Queen of England, or else the king of someplace nobody ever heard of, like Utopia."

"Where's that?"

"I don't know," I said. "But I read about it in a book, so it's got to be somewhere."

We finished off the handbills and went back to the van. After that there was nothing much to do but loaf around and finish off the food wrapped in the oilcloth. We were good and tired and turned in as soon as it got dark.

In the morning the Professor got out a cloth sign saying:

PROFESSOR ALBERTO SANTINI SAVANT OF
THE HEALING ARTS

We helped him rig it up across the front of the van. Then he said, "I don't suppose either of you fellas is any good at singing and dancing."

"I can sing a little," I said. I could sing better than Billy, anyway. "But they didn't have a whole lot of dancing at the Home."

"Play the banjo?"

We shook our heads. "I figured as much. Well, we'll have to do the best we can." He went into the van, rummaged around a little, and came out with a horn and a couple of white nightshirts with all sorts of strange designs in green on them—flashes of lighting, a scale, a snake, dice. "Here, put these on. I got to make a grand entrance. Got to impress these here hicks. Billy, you know how to drive a mule?"

"Some," he said. He didn't have the faintest idea of mules, but he wasn't going to miss out on his chance. It was just like I feared: he saw he was cut out for this business and wanted to get in on everything. I could tell the Professor saw it, too, and would encourage Billy in it.

"All right, Billy. You climb up there and drive us into town." He handed me the horn. "Possum, you go along in front blowing on this horn. When we get into town, pull up in Courthouse Square and circulate among the throng, passing out handbills."

He climbed into the van, and off we went, me tooting out a kind of rusty noise on that horn, and Billy cursing and shouting at the mules, which had a habit of stopping every five minutes to snatch a bite of tasty dandelions. Every time they did that, the Professor would shout from inside the van, "Give them a lick with the whip, Billy. I thought you said you could handle mules." But Billy didn't know any more about handling a whip than he did mules, and he spent half the time tangled up in it when he wasn't poking himself in the eye with the butt end.

We came into town. I felt like a fool in that nightshirt, making rusty noises on that horn, but luckily there weren't all that many people around—not what you'd call a throng. We went on down the main street and into Courthouse Square. There wasn't much of a throng here, either—about six or eight farmers in overalls and straw hats clustered on the sidewalk.

Luckily, just as we got abreast of them, the mules stopped of their own accord. Billy wiped off his face with the hem of his nightshirt, and then we went amongst the people passing out the handbills. That entertainment lasted about three minutes. We went back to the van and stood side by side, trying to look like we knew what we were doing. I felt as foolish as could be and kept blushing, which made things even worse. I wished the Professor would hurry up and come out so's there wouldn't be so much attention on us, but he took his time. Pretty soon a couple more people drifted over, then two or three more, until the crowd had got up to fifteen or twenty.

Finally the Professor came out. He had put on a frock coat over his regular clothes and over the top of that a red sash covered with medals running diagonally across his chest. He made a bow to the audience and climbed up on the driver's seat. Taking a bottle of the elixir out of the coat pocket, he held it up and began to spiel, talking in some kind of accent that would have made me bust out laughing if I hadn't of been so embarrassed. He told them how happy he was to be visiting the charming town of Sabbath and how intelligent the citizens all were. Then he went into the wonderful properties of the elixir, naming all the things it would cure, which was just about anything. He told a couple of stories of famous people who he'd cured with it—Billy's king of France wasn't so far off the mark, even if France didn't have a king. He told them nowhere else could you buy human happiness for a dollar a bottle.

It was beyond me how he could get up there dressed like a circus ringmaster and sling out that palaver in that fake accent. I couldn't of done it for a million dollars—I'd of dropped dead of shame.

But Billy was just the opposite. He stood there with his mouth open, staring and taking it all in. From time to time I saw his lips move, like he was trying out something the Professor said. Oh, I was going to have a time of it dragging him off to look for the lake of gold.

Finally the Professor said, "My assistants will now pass among you a sample bottle. Just taste it for yourself and see if you don't feel much improved on the instant."

We each took a bottle of the stuff and went amongst the little crowd. They were curious, by and large, and most of them took a sip—pretty careful, once they got a smell of it. One or two even said, "By golly, I do feel perked up a little," which didn't surprise me, for that taste would of waked up a dead man. Finally someone bit. That started the thing rolling, and before you knew it we'd sold seven or eight bottles and had three or four more people wavering.

And the Professor was just starting on another spiel to see if he couldn't pull the waverers across the line, when somebody just behind us said in a voice so loud we jumped: "As I suspected, Johnny McCarthy."

Me and Billy whipped around, and the Professor broke off his spiel. Standing just a bit back from the van so he was facing the crowd was a fella in a suit, tie, and brown derby hat. He took a big gold watch out of his pocket, snapped the lid up, and looked at it. "I'll give you just ten minutes to get you and your little trolls out of town."

He snapped the lid of the watch closed and stuck it back in his pocket.

We looked up at the Professor. He swiveled around to face the man. "Sir, you must be mistaken. I'm Professor Alberto Santini of the—"

"Ten minutes, Johnny." He unbuttoned his suit jacket and let it fall open. We could now see a small pistol tucked into the waist of his pants. He turned and walked away.

The Professor turned back to the little mob. "Sorry about the intrusion, folks. Pay no attention." He gestured to me, and I came back into the van. He bent over. "Quick, see if you can sell a couple more bottles." He started spieling again. We went back into the crowd and did sell two more bottles. Then, out of the corner of my eye, I saw the man in the suit and the derby hat strolling toward us again. The Professor waved to us. "I'm sorry we must say good-bye. It brings a tear to the eyes to have to leave your charming town, but we have a great many places to visit." He sat down on the van seat and picked up the reins. "Quick, boys, hop aboard." He picked up the whip, gave the mules a lick, and in a minute we were heading on out the opposite side of Courthouse Square into the country-side beyond. As we rumbled onto the dirt road, I took a look back at the man in the suit and derby hat. He was standing alone in the middle of the square, one hand cradling the watch, the other hand on the butt of the pistol.

Chapter Seven

We skipped through the next two or three little towns in order to get well clear of the gent with the pistol, the watch, and the derby hat. Finally we pulled down a wood lane, where we were clear of the road. The Professor sent us off to find firewood and a stream, and as soon as we were out of earshot I said, "I knew it, Billy. I knew sooner or later we'd get into trouble, and here it happened on our second day. We've got to get away from this Professor and find other jobs."

He put his hands on his hips and puffed out his cheeks. "I didn't think you were such a coward, Possum. That fella wasn't going to shoot anybody. He was just threatening us. Probably has his own game going in Sabbath and didn't want us moving in on him. Did you get a look at him? He wasn't any farmer in overalls and a straw hat. He was up to something."

"Don't bother calling me a coward, Billy. I didn't see you looking so blame happy when that fella came around with that little pistol."

"We already left that fella thirty miles behind us."

"Still, I don't see any reason for being shot at when we don't have to be. We're supposed to be hunting for that gold lake, not running around the country skinning people," I said.

"Where else are we going to get a job like this? No work to amount to anything, good grub, lots of time to lie around in the sun, and a dollar a day besides."

"Yes, a dollar a day would be mighty good money if we ever saw any of it."

"Oh, he'll pay us, Possum. He's got to sooner or later."

"I'll believe it when I see it."

He frowned. Then he said, "All right, Possum, you got another job for us?"

He had me there. "Well, OK, I can see where we've got to stick to this for a while. Once we get some money saved up, we go look for that lake."

He didn't say anything, but I knew he was thinking that if he could just get me to stick with it for a bit, I'd get used to it.

For the next week we traipsed along in that van from one little town to the next—West Potato, Harpoon, Misery Plains, Dead Creek. There wasn't much to choose from amongst them—same main street, same grain-and-feed store, same dogs laying in the same dusty street, same farmers in overalls and straw hats leaning somewhere chewing straw. Sometimes we did pretty good and sold a couple of dozen bottles of the elixir, sometimes only six or seven. It was enough to get along on—buy oats for the mules, eggs, meat, potatoes, and cider for the humans, kerosene, shoe polish, and such for the business. The Professor kept saying, "Never mind, boys. We're just warming up. Down the road there's some big towns where we'll clean up."

I figured the Professor was stowing away a little money for himself, for he did all the shopping. We could figure how much was coming in pretty close, but we didn't know how much was going out. All we ever knew was what the Professor told us, and that was usually on the order of, "I never heard of such a price for kerosene," or "that fella must think them eggs is gold-plated," usually with a shake of the head.

There was one thing to be said for the Professor, though: he liked his chow. He could cook good, too, even though it was over a campfire and he had only three or four pots and pans to work with. He took a lot of pains over it. "See here, fellas, how them eggs is just beginning to get a shine on top? Now you baste it with the hot fat, and in half a minute they'll be done just right—the white hard and the yellow still runny enough to soak into the bread." He'd fry up slices of bread in the fat, and you'd have the best tasting fried-egg sandwiches you ever slid into your mouth. Same thing with everything else—steak done just so; fried potatoes crisp but not hard; pancakes golden brown, firm but moist inside. Billy was beginning to fill out, and he said I was, too. If they'd had cooking like that at the Home, we might never of run off.

Billy was having the time of his life. He'd lost interest in that gold lake.

He was getting some idea of handling mules, although they were still suspicious of him and would balk on him sometimes. He was practicing up on the Professor's spiel—I wasn't supposed to know that, but sometimes I'd see his lips moving while the Professor was throwing his line. And he'd graduated from hauling water up to helping the Professor mix the elixir. "You're doing right good, Billy," the Professor said. "You got a ways to go, but you'll get there. I don't doubt that the time'll come when I'll be able to turn the mixing over to you altogether." That didn't surprise me very much: the Professor was usually ready to turn over to us anything he could.

I noticed another thing, too: I was getting used to it myself. The days were beginning to blur together and so were all those people we were skinning. They weren't people anymore, just hands waving dollars at us.

The more I saw that, the more it worried me. Back at the Home, we boys figured we deserved anything we could get away with. Out here it was getting harder and harder for me to see where these people deserved to be skinned. Oh, some of them did: the Professor said so, and I didn't doubt it. But some of them—you could tell by their clothes and such—needed their dollar as much as the Professor did. They only gave it up because they were desperate to cure their husband or their old ma of something. It was making me wonder.

I brought it up with Billy one afternoon when we were walking into some little town to put up a poster.

"Billy, what about that lake?"

"Shucks," he said. "I figured you'd probably forgotten all about it."

"Well, I haven't. We agreed we'd stick it out with the Professor until we saved up some money, and then we'd go find the lake."

"I don't know where I agreed to that."

"Yes, you did, Billy." To tell the truth, I couldn't remember exactly what he'd agreed to that last time we'd talked about it, but I figured he didn't, either.

He paused. Then he said, "That's just it, Possum. We haven't saved up any money."

"That's because the Professor hasn't given us any. He owes us for a week. He's got us doing most of the work now, except for the spiel and jamming dollar bills in his pants. He's just bone lazy, Billy."

"Possum, I hate to quit now, just when I'm beginning to get the hang of spieling. I'd like to get to where I could do it myself." He gave me a look. "It might come in handy for us someday."

73

"No, it won't, Billy. More likely we'll get shot by somebody we skinned once too often."

"Oh, don't worry about that fella, Possum. He's long behind us."

"Still, you agreed," I said.

He stood there frowning and trying to remember what he'd agreed to. "I don't think I ever agreed in just so many words," he said.

That was probably true. Billy was likely to be pretty cagey about exactly what he agreed to. But he didn't remember for sure. "Billy, you agreed."

He shook his head, sore at himself because he couldn't remember. "That may be so," he said finally. "But we still haven't got any money."

"We got to ask him for it," I said.

"He might not like it."

"I don't reckon he's going to like it," I said. "But if we don't ask him, we'll never get it."

It was clear that Billy didn't really care about the money: it was the easy life and skinning people that he liked. But he couldn't admit that—he had to pretend he was in it for the money. "All right, Possum, I agree we got to get our money. But you got to ask him for it, since it was your idea."

The idea made me nervous, for I knew that the Professor would be sore about it. What would I do if he told me to beat it, that he and Billy would run the business without me? Would Billy let me go like that? I didn't think he would, so the Professor would have to be careful about what he said. Still, it made me nervous.

I waited until supper, when the Professor was feeling contented and had nothing better to do with himself but sit there burping his chicken and biscuits. I tried to think of a soft way of putting it, but I couldn't, so I plunged in.

"Prof, it's been a week since we came onboard. When do you figure you might give us our money?"

The Professor gave me a look and frowned. "I'm mighty sorry you felt you had to bring that up, Possum. It don't show much faith in old Prof, does it? Especially not after I rescued you and Billy from that Home and got you started out in a trade most young fellas would give their right arm for." He put on a sorrowful expression, like he was Saint Christopher with the weight of the world on his shoulders, and stared up at the sky. Finally he said, "I'll tell you what I'm going to do, Possum. I'm going to forgive you. Yes, I'm going to take into account that you was raised in a Home without a ma's tender arms around you, and you got hard and greedy from the experience. I'm going to find compassion in my heart for you and do like a good Christian—forgive." He swiveled his head down from the sky and looked at me. "There. Enough said, Possum. We'll just forget the whole thing. We'll consider you never said anything about it."

He was spieling me just the way he did the folks with the elixir, and it made me sore. "Prof, you said you'd pay us a dollar a day."

Billy jumped in. "That's right, Prof. You didn't rescue us from the Home. I blame near killed myself sliding out that window." Billy knew there wouldn't be any excuse for staying if we didn't get the money.

Now it was Billy's turn to receive the sorrowful Saint Christopher look. "So that's all the thanks I get, Billy. I didn't want to tell you this, for I didn't want to worry you both none. But that Deacon of yours was right on your trail. I saw him myself coming along the street peering this way and that way down the alleys and into doorways."

"I wonder how you recognized him," I said.

"Recognize him? Why I didn't have to recognize him. He came right up to me and asked did I see a couple of raggedy boys that had run away from a Home? There was a hundred-dollar reward out, cash on the barrelhead. Did I turn you in? Nothing of the kind. I said I had just got into town myself and didn't see any boys. You fellas had better think twice before you scoff at what I done for you."

There wasn't a word of truth in it. Deacon would never, ever put up a hundred dollars reward even if his own sister got kidnapped out of the Home. I was determined he wasn't going to skin us. "Even so," I said, "we got to have some money. We can't go on working for nothing forever."

He raised his eyes up to the sky once more, like he was begging the saints to help him bear it. Then he looked back at us. "Fellas, you don't understand the amount of expenses we run to each day. This business don't run on air. It takes money. Some days we don't even make expenses."

"Still, there's got to be a few dollars left over. What's the point of us being in a business if we can't get anything out of it?"

"Possum's right, Prof. You got to pay us something."

Prof pursed his lips. "Well, I tell you what, boys. I can see nothing I say is going to touch your greedy little hearts. Suppose we make it a dollar each. A dollar's a lot of money for boys your age."

"You said a dollar a day."

He picked up a stick and started scratching in the dirt by the fire, like he was adding up the numbers. "All right, I guess I could find two dollars each. But that's as far as she'll stretch."

"Five dollars," I said.

"You're breaking my heart, Possum. After everything I done for you, practically working my fingers to the bone just to see you got some decent grub for a change. Make it three dollars."

"Four," I said.

"Split the difference," he said. "Three-fifty each."

But of course in the end he said he didn't have the right change, and we got three dollars and a quarter each. He was careful to turn his back to us when he counted the dollars off his roll of bills. Still, we'd get some of it. That was the first time in my life I ever had any money of my own. Three dollars and a quarter seemed like a fortune. Oh, it was a glorious feeling, all right, to have that much money. I wasn't thinking about what I could buy with it. In fact, the last thing I wanted to do was spend it. I just wanted to have it.

But now that we'd got some money, I was stuck with staying with the Professor for a while. We didn't have enough money to branch off on our own; Billy'd make me stay with it until we did. I'd sort of trapped myself.

A couple of days later, we came over a rise and saw below us, a few miles along, one of those big towns the Professor had been talking bout. Even at a distance we could see that it was more than just a main street. It had four or five streets running one way and four or five more running across them. I counted three church steeples and some kind of stone courthouse, too.

But there was something else in the view that took my breath away. In the distance was a line of mountains—not hills, but real mountains. I kind of shuddered from excitement. "Look, Billy."

"You think it's them?"

"I don't know." Prof was standing by the van staring down into the town like it was the Promised Land and the Lord was parting the Red Sea for him. "Prof, is that Plunket City?"

"Why, yes, Possum. How'd you know that?"

"Somebody told me about it." So there it was: somewhere up in those mountains was that lake full of gold.

We pulled the van off into a stand of trees by the road. Prof set Billy to unhitching the mules and currying them and sent me into town with a dollar to buy supper. "Have a good stroll around, Possum. See what you can see. I got to do some heavy thinking. There's good pickings in that town if I can come up with the right idea." Going off by myself was just what I wanted to do. He sat down with his back against a tree, pulled off his boots and closed his eyes so he could see all the stuff flying around inside his head better. I reckoned he'd be sound asleep before I was a quarter mile down the road.

I set off, and by and by I came to a sprinkling of houses along the road. In a bit the road turned into a cobble street, and I was going along a wood sidewalk with a good many shops and stores, mingled with some nice houses. There were plenty of people, too. Somebody would know about those mountains. So I sauntered along, looking around at this and that, just taking in the sights, when I came across that stone building I'd seen from the rise. It was three stories high, with a clock tower in the roof, and carved across the front in stone letters was PLUNKET CITY TOWN HALL.

Somebody in there was bound to know all about those mountains. It made me a little nervous to go in there and ask: suppose I wasn't allowed. But I'd never find out about those mountains if I didn't ask, so I took a deep breath, marched up the town-hall steps, swung the door open, and went in.

It was nice and cool in there. I was in a corridor with doors all along it—county sheriff, tax assessor, department of public works, and such. I ought to stay away from the sheriff; that was clear. I didn't even know what a tax assessor was, but I figured I'd better stay away from him, too. The department of public works sounded safer. I went up to the door. I didn't know if you were supposed to knock or just go in, so to be safe I knocked. Nothing happened. I pushed the door open. There was a railing across the front of the room, a couple of people waiting in chairs in front of the railing, and behind the railing three or four people at work at desks. I sat down in a chair to wait my turn. Next to me was a farmer in overalls, smoking a corn-cob pipe. "I hope I'm not bothering you, but I was wondering about those mountains out there." I certainly wasn't going to admit about the golden lake.

He looked me over. "Ain't much to wonder about," he said finally. "They're mountains."

"Well, yes, I can see that. I was wondering what kind of mountains they are. What they're called and all."

He thought about it for a minute. "Blame if I know what they're called. Don't have any special name, I reckon. Around here they just call them the mountains."

"If you wanted to go up there, are there any trails and such?"

"Folks don't go up there too much. Easy to get lost. Lots of fellas has went up there and never was seen again. Some folks says they put a spell on people deliberate. Every time you turn your head, things look different. Don't believe in spells myself, but there might be something to it. I knew a fella who went up in there twenty years ago and still ain't come out." He looked me over again. "You fixin' on going up there?"

"No," I said, getting excited again, for it sounded like the right mountains. "I'm new around here. I was curious is all."

Then I realized that the door to the office was open, and a man was standing there, watching me and listening. He was wearing a suit and tie and a gold watch chain across from one side of his vest to the other. He hadn't got the pistol in his belt, but I figured he could lay his hands on it pretty quick if he wanted to.

I got hot and sweaty, and my heart began to race. I was giving myself away, but I couldn't help it. I turned back to the farmer with the corncob pipe. "I don't suppose you know of any jobs around here? My pa and ma died, and I'm trying to get back east to live with my uncle Will. But I ran out of money." It sounded pretty limp to me—I wished I had Billy along to do the lying.

The man stepped into the room and closed the door behind him. I knew I oughtn't to pay him any attention, but I couldn't help giving him a quick look.

I said to the farmer, "That's why I came in here. I figured they might have some jobs with the public works."

Then I realized that the man with the gold watch chain was standing right over me, staring down. "So," he said, "Johnny McCarthy's in town."

I looked up at him, trying not to blush. "You talking to me, sir?"

"I'm talking to you, yes. Where's McCarthy?"

"Sir, I don't know anyone named McCarthy. I don't know anyone at all around here."

His hand shot out, and he grabbed ahold of my shirt front. The cloth was old and faded, and I could hear it give when he jerked me to my feet. "Sir, I don't know—"

He gave me a shake. "Now you listen to me, you little skunk. You tell McCarthy I want him out of this town as fast as he can skedaddle. If I see him anywhere pulling his skin game, he's going to be mighty sorry he ever crossed the city line. Am I clear?"

There wasn't anything else for me to say. He let me go, and I ran out of there, leaving the door open behind me. I dashed down the wide town-hall steps and headed back toward where I'd come from, every once in a while looking over my shoulder to see if anyone was chasing me.

Chapter Eight

The whole thing shook me a good deal, and I forgot all about buying supper. But when I brought the news back to the Professor, it kind of took away his appetite, and we made do with some bread and cheese. Prof didn't say much while we were eating—"pass the mustard" and such. But I figured we had a right to know, as we were in it, too. "Who is he, Prof?" I said.

He frowned so deep his eyebrows almost touched. "Fella name of Robinson. Harper Robinson. Surveyor by trade. That's why you came upon him in the works department. Laying out a water line or a piece of property somewhere, most probably. He ain't from up around here. Comes from a place south a hundred miles. Town called Deep Creek. He travels on the surveying business all the time, so you're likely to come across him anywhere in these parts. See, suppose a fella down in Deep Creek wants to speculate in land up here, he's going to send his own surveyor out, and not go by a local one who might be a friend of the seller and lay out the land a few acres short."

"What's he got against you?" Billy said.

"Oh well." He sat there thinking about it for a while, hunched together, his whole face moving in the direction of his nose. Finally he picked up a stick from the ground and began playing around in the campfire coals with it. "It was an accident. I don't see why he had to blame me for it. It wasn't like I did it on purpose. He might as well take it out on God, for He had a hand in it, too—more'n I did, surely. Like I say, it was an accident."

"But what happened, Prof?" I said.

"I came into this here Deep Creek. I had a little thing going that I called Bailey's Baby Powders. It wasn't anything but cornstarch with brown sugar and spices mixed in—nutmeg, cinnamon, and such—so the kids would beg for it. Mix a teaspoon in their milk. Folks go for anything that shuts their babies up awhile. There was a lot of diphtheria going around down there at that time, which was why I was pushing the baby powders. There wasn't any harm in it—a kid could eat a box of it and wouldn't be hurt. Do the kid some good, like as not."

"Were you working alone, Prof?'

"No, no. I had this fella with me—half Indian, half Mexican. Fastest hand at spotting the suckers in a crowd I ever did see."

"What was his trick?" Billy said. He was jealous, and he wanted to know the secret of it.

"Let's come back to that," I said. "I want to hear about this Robinson."

"Where was I?"

"Selling baby powders."

"Yes. We was out there in Deep Creek, me and this fella, selling baby powders. This young couple came up, carrying a little girl. Well, not so little, maybe three, four years old. Cutest little thing I ever saw. Head full of curls, shiny brown eyes. But mighty sick, too. Well, of course, they was real worried about her, said she'd got a fever and moaned all night, would the powders do any good. Well, I was kind of stuck. There was a lot of people gathered around, and I couldn't hardly say the powders wasn't anything but cornstarch and sugar, for I'd just spent a half hour telling everybody how good they was. So I said they was the best thing in the world. And that's where I made my mistake."

He sat there kind of brooding over it for a bit. Me and Billy kept quiet, and finally he began again. "What I should of done was tell 'em to take the kid to a doc just to be on the safe side. That's what I usually did in these cases. I don't mind killing some old farmer now and again who hasn't done anything for mankind but chew straw and spit on his shoes for forty years. But I kind of draw the line at kids. This time it got away from me. A couple of people jumped in with questions, and by the time I got back to the young couple this

Indian fella had sold them the powders and they'd gone home.

"Well, there wasn't anything I could do about it, and I put it out of my mind. I figured if they had any sense they'd take the kid to a doc anyway, and then it'd be on his conscience, not mine, if she died. But they didn't. They put all their faith in those powders, and blamed if four days later she didn't die. Of course I didn't know anything about it—I was three towns away. But it turned out she was this here Robinson's little granddaughter. He tucked that pistol in his waist-band and came looking for me. He caught me spieling in front of a mob of people. He turned my face against the van and put the pistol to my head. I figured I was a dead man. Stood there waiting for the crash, trying to say the Lord's Prayer, but so scared I couldn't get past the first line. Then he said he would of shot me, but his daughter had another one on the way, and she needed him out of jail. But he beat me up around the head pretty good with that pistol. And he said if he ever caught me spieling again, he'd shoot me where I stood. Now, in fact, he ain't likely to shoot me in front of a crowd—sure to go to jail for that, and maybe hang in the bargain. But I wouldn't want him to catch me out in the woods."

I sat there feeling cold and sick with myself. What if somebody I'd sold Thurman's Elixir to had already died? Maybe they had. We'd sold plenty of it to people for their kids. I knew that, for they'd come up and say their kid had this or that wrong with him, was the Elixir any good for it. When that happened, I was on the spot. I didn't want to say it was good for anything, but I couldn't say it wasn't, not after the Professor had been saying how wonderful it was. Usually I said something like, "Lots of folks have bought it for their kids." I saw now that was almost worse than telling people straight out that the stuff would cure anything—worse because it was just a way for me to feel better about lying to them. I sat there feeling just plain awful. "Maybe you should have quit the business," I said in a low voice.

"I did for a while. For one thing, my face was so cut up I didn't dare go out in public. But after a month it healed. I figured the whole thing would die down and I'd go back to it."

His face wasn't scrunched up anymore, but had got back to normal, like it had made him feel better to get the whole thing off his chest. But he looked kind of sad, too. "What else could I do? I spent my life spieling. It's the only thing I'm good at. When I was young, I tried my hand at a lot of things—driving mules, clerking in a department store. I even worked in a bank for a bit. None of it went too good. Driving mules was hard work—too hard for me. Clerking bored me to death. As for banking, by the end of the first week, I knew I'd never last. All that money there just waiting to be took was more than I could stand. Gobs of it, stacks of tens and twenties and fifties, crisp and new, and the prettiest sight I ever saw. I was so keyed up I had to keep swallering all the time. By the end of the second week I was twitching so bad I could hardly pick up a pen. I knew I had to quit, or I'd be in jail." He shook his head. "No, boys, the only thing that ever worked for me was spieling. I didn't have no choice. So I went back to it. But I was mighty careful to stay out of that county where Robinson lives. What I didn't reckon on was him being a surveyor and traveling around so much. This makes the third time he's come across my trail."

He sat there staring into the coals of the campfire, from time to time poking them with the stick to send up sparks. "It ain't right," he said finally. "It ain't fair. I never killed that little girl on purpose. Probably she would of died anyway. Robinson's got no business chasing me around like that. A man's got a right to make a living, ain't he?" He left off poking the coals with the stick and glared across at us. "Where's Robinson come off telling me I can't work this here town?"

The thing that bothered me most about it was that he didn't seem sorry about the little girl. The only thing that interested him was throwing the blame off on God and steering clear of Robinson. It was himself he was sorry for.

Maybe it was time I branched off. Why couldn't I? There wasn't any reason for it that I could see. It was just my feelings. Why should I feel so strong about not branching off from Billy? I couldn't explain it to myself. Well, feelings or not, if he wouldn't quit now, I was gone. I took a glance at Billy and saw he'd been looking at me. He knew what I was thinking, and he said quickly, "Prof, let's skip Plunket City. It isn't worth the risk."

He shook his head. "No, Billy, this here town's a gold mine. It's the first real place we hit so far. We could sell a hundred, two hundred, five hundred bottles in a place like this. I know; I've done it. We can go sailing out of here with a sackful of money and our pockets crammed, too. You could each earn twenty bucks in this place in an afternoon." He gave the fire a hard jab with the stick, sending a stream of sparks up into the night. "No, by glory, I'm not going to let Robinson run me out of here. He's got no right. If he starts anything, I'll holler for the sheriff. It's a free country, ain't it?"

There was no arguing with him, I could see that. I figured the best thing was to get a night's sleep and hope that he'd calm down a little in the morning and would listen to reason. Then when we'd got safe into another town where me and Billy could find jobs, we'd tell him he was on his own.

So we bedded down, and as soon as the Professor flung his clothes into the van and climbed in after them I said, "Billy, we got to get out of this. What if we already killed somebody?"

"Possum, we haven't killed anybody. We'd of heard of it. Besides, if anybody did die, they most likely were bound to die, anyway."

"Billy, I'm not going to get talked into it anymore. I'm going to quit. You remember, we were supposed to be looking for that golden lake."

He leaned up on his elbow. I could see his face from the low glow of the fire. "Stop thinking about people dying, Possum. You worry too much. Think about all those dollar bills stuffed in our pockets."

"It isn't worth it, Billy. I'm through."

"You can't quit now, Possum. Not when we're about to hit it rich."

"Nope. I made up my mind, Billy. I'm through. You can go down into that town with Prof. I'm not going to."

He didn't say anything. We looked at each other in the firelight. "You really mean it? You'd skip all those dollar bills?"

"I really mean it, Billy."

He lay back and stared up through the trees to where a few stars peeked through. "Well, all right, Possum. If you say we got to quit, we'll quit. Maybe you're right. Maybe we ought to be in those mountains looking for that lake. This medicine game would be mighty small potatoes compared with a lake full of gold."

"Then you'll quit with me, Billy?"

"I'll make you a deal, Possum. We'll do it this one last time. Stuff our pockets full of money so we don't have to worry for a while and then head for the mountains."

I didn't want to do it, not even one last time. I just wanted to get up in the morning and leave Prof, the mules, and the elixir behind. Suppose this was the time when we actually got somebody killed. But I had to agree, for it was a fair bargain. "All right," I said. "It's a deal."

In the morning, while we were drinking our coffee and chewing what was left of the bread—it had got pretty tough—I tried to talk the Professor into skipping Plunket City. I couldn't do it. He'd got it fixed in his mind that he wasn't going to let Robinson push him around anymore. "He'll back down. You'll see, boys. These here bullies are all the same—stand up to them and they back down."

"What if he doesn't, Prof?" I said.

He shifted his eyes to one side. "He better."

So we mixed up the elixir, stretched the sign across the wagon, and around eleven o'clock me and Billy went into town to paste up the handbills. We spent an awful lot of time looking over our shoulders for a sight of Robinson, for I'd made up my mind that if the Professor wanted to back him down, that was his lookout; but as for me, I was going to run like the wind. However, he didn't turn up.

We picked up some ham and rolls for lunch and went on back to the van. At two o'clock we set off for town, me and Billy dressed in those blame nightshirts, me out front tooting that horn. I was thankful for one thing, at least: it was the last time I'd ever have to put on that shirt and toot that horn.

Billy had got a little better handle on the mules—at least he wasn't poking himself in the eye with the whip handle as frequent. We sailed into town and set up in the square in front of the town hall—just the exact place where Robinson was most likely to turn up. I figured the Professor did it deliberate, just to show he wasn't going to be pushed around.

But no Robinson; I figured he was out in the countryside doing some surveying. So we set to work.

It turned out that the Professor was right about the place being a gold mine. We pulled a crowd of a couple hundred people, way bigger than any crowd we ever had. And maybe even larger than that, for they kept coming and going. Me and Billy were taking in those dollar bills as fast as we could stuff them in our pockets. Prof was mighty set up about the way the money was coming in, but he was a lot happier when the money was in his pockets, not ours; and every little while he'd jump off the van seat, where he was spieling, reach into our pockets, and haul out a fistful of bills.

Things had just begun to slow down a little, with Prof trying to coax a few more dollars out of the crowd, when that familiar voice slammed out behind me: "Johnny McCarthy."

Me and Billy jumped around. Robinson was standing behind the van, a little off to one side. His coat was open so's we could see the butt of his pistol. "McCarthy," he shouted again.

The Professor turned his head around and gave Robinson a kind of sneer. Then he turned back to the crowd. "Sorry for the interruption, folks. Don't pay it no mind. We just got a few bottles of this famous elixir left. When they're gone, that's it. I want to remind you of the tremendous curative powers of this here—"

But me and Billy weren't listening. We were staring at Robinson like mice trapped by a cat. He put his hand on the butt of the pistol. We dove headfirst under the van and lay flat. Robinson pulled out the pistol and, aiming it into the air, fired.

The crack was as loud as thunder, and it got the Professor's attention. From where we lay we couldn't see him, but it was clear he turned around to face Robinson, for he said, "I ain't scared of you, Robinson. You got no right to interfere with my business. This is a free country."

"Free country or not, Johnny . . ." He fumbled his watch out with his left hand and snapped the case open. "I'm giving you one minute to pick up those reins and haul that van out of here. Otherwise, I'm going to shoot you where you stand."

Now the throng was busting up, with the people scattering in all directions—racing to the sides of the square, babbling and squealing. But not the Professor. "You don't scare me none, Robinson. I got my rights."

We couldn't see Prof, but we could see Robinson all right. He was standing there cool as you please, holding the pistol loose in one hand, and every few seconds taking a look at the watch. "Thirty seconds, Johnny."

The square was now empty, with the crowd around the edges, mostly kneeling, not wanting to miss it if Robinson killed Prof, but ready to make a run for it if bullets started whizzing in their direction.

"Ten seconds, Johnny. One, two—"

"You wouldn't dare. I'm going to call the sheriff to protect my rights."

Robinson raised the pistol. "I warned you, Johnny." He fired. The Professor let out a kind of squeal, but that was the last we knew of it, for me and Billy were flying across the empty square as fast as we could move, flinging off those nightshirts as we went.

Chapter Nine

We ran through the streets of that town like we were being chased by demons set on sending us to Hell for eternity. Our lungs burned and our legs ached, but we went on running—past shopwindows, past mule wagons and dogs that jumped up out of the dusty street and barked as we sailed by. People turned their heads to stare at us, and a few of them shouted "hey" at us, for they judged we'd been up to some mischief. But we were by them before they could stop us. On we went until we came to the outskirts of town, where there were no more shops, only houses and barns, the cobblestone street turned to dirt.

We stood by the side of the road, gasping for air, wiping the sweat from our faces with our sleeves. Our legs were trembling, and I don't believe either of us could have taken another step even if we saw real demons streaming toward us. Finally we got ourselves pulled together and started off down the road at a walk, looking back over our shoulders from time to time, just in case. "Do you think Robinson killed Prof?" Billy said.

It was mighty scary to think of Prof being dead—standing on that van seat spieling away only twenty minutes ago and now lying there with his eyes open but not seeing anything. It gave me a feeling of awe to have somebody I knew be dead. He wasn't a perfect fella—you couldn't say that. But he had his likable side. It was interesting to hear him talk, even if you couldn't believe much of what he said. He'd been alive, and it got me to thinking what it meant to be alive—to breathe, argue with people, fry potatoes and eggs, and walk and twist and bend. He was there, and now maybe he wasn't there anymore. "He could of just got wounded," I said. "Or maybe Robinson missed him completely."

Billy shook his head. "He wouldn't of missed. He was standing too close."

"Well, maybe he missed on purpose. Maybe he was afraid to shoot him with all those witnesses standing around."

"I hope so," Billy said. "I hate to think he's dead. I got to where I liked him. Of course you couldn't trust him as far as you could throw him. But you can't trust me, either. Look what I did—tried to steal his purse out of his pants ten minutes after I promised I wouldn't."

"It was more like five minutes," I said.

"Don't exaggerate, Possum. I wasted five minutes trying to talk myself out of it."

I didn't want to get into it. "Well, Billy, some good came out of it. We're a long ways from the Home, and we got three dollars and a quarter in our pockets. Besides, you haven't stolen anything for a while."

He grinned. "I wouldn't say that. Look." He reached into his back pocket and pulled out a bunch of dollar bills crunched up in a wad.

"Blame me," I said. "Where'd you get all that?"

"From selling the elixir back there. I kept two pockets going, one Prof knew about and one he didn't know about. As the money came in, I divided it between the two pockets."

I should have figured it. To be honest, I was glad to see that wad of dollar bills. Three dollars and a quarter each wouldn't have kept us going very long, and I didn't have any idea how long it would take us to get up into those mountains and find that lake full of gold. Still, I wondered. What were the rights and wrongs of it? Was it OK to steal money that was already being stolen? Especially when we were helping to steal it? Of course the Professor would never admit he was skinning people. His line was, "If they're dumb enough to be took advantage of, that's their lookout. It's the American way—*caveat empty*. That's Latin. It means it's the buyer's lookout if he comes away empty-handed." To my mind, that line didn't follow. Why was it the other fella's fault that you were skinning him? It seemed to me you had to take part of the blame yourself. But that wasn't the way the Professor thought.

Anyway, whatever the rights and wrongs of it, I was glad to see the money. "Well, I don't know as I blame you, Billy. I wouldn't have done it, but all the same, he never paid us what he owed us."

"That's right," Billy said. "But it wouldn't have mattered to me if he had." He looked at me, grinning, his eyes shining. "I believe in stealing. It suits my nature."

"You don't have to tell me that," I said. "I just hope you don't get us both put in jail."

"Nah," he said. "I won't get caught."

"You got caught plenty back at the Home."

"Deacon, he was bound to catch you, for he'd whip you for no reason, so whatever you did, you'd get caught."

Billy had a way of twisting things around so's he was in the right of it. He was mighty smart. But I wasn't always sure what he said was true, even though it sounded right. "Let's see the money, Billy. How much is it?"

He hunkered down and, one by one, uncrumpled the dollar bills and stacked them on the ground. When he got them all straightened out as much as he could, he counted them out. Then he whistled. "Twenty-two dollars."

"Blame me," I said.

He picked up the money and cou[...]
bills. "Here," he said. "Here's your half[...]

"Hey," I said. "You don't need to[...]
didn't steal it—you stole it."

"Here, take it, Possum. I wouldn'[...]
keeping it all myself."

I looked at him, shaking my head. "Billy, some-times I just can't understand you. You got the blamedest way of thinking I ever saw. Here you'll stick your hand in somebody's pocket, but once you get the money, you're bound and determined to give it away."

"That's just the way I am, Possum. I don't care about the money so much. What interests me is steal-ing it. Once I got it stole, somebody else can have it."

I folded the bills and stuck them into my pocket. We would need money for food along the way, and I reckoned we'd be better off if I took care of some of it. "Do you think you're going to give away all the money we get for that gold?"

"I don't know what I'll do with the money," Billy said. "Maybe I'll buy a van and go traveling around the countryside. What about that for an idea, Possum?"

"Not me," I said. "No more vans for me. You know what I was thinking of?"

"What?"

I kind of hesitated, for I figured he might laugh at me. "I was thinking about buying the Home off Deacon and letting the boys run it themselves the way they want to."

He didn't laugh, for he saw I was serious and didn't want to hurt my feelings. "That's okay, Possum. Me, I wouldn't waste any money on those kids. They're mostly no good, anyway. But maybe you'd have some left over for yourself."

"I reckon there's going to be plenty," I said. I felt sort of embarrassed to talk about it. "We better get going," I said.

We were lucky in one thing, for we happened to run out the side of Plunket City toward the mountains. They were dead ahead of us, rising up into the sky, kind of hazy purple. There were three of them in a row—or maybe you'd say it was one mountain with three peaks.

We started off walking toward them. "How far do you think they are, Possum?" Billy said.

"A good piece, I reckon. Probably farther than they look. Ten miles, anyway."

"That's not so bad," Billy said. "We could get there by nightfall, maybe."

We walked on. We were now well clear of town and into farm country. Cornfields all around us, here and there a field of hay or a woodlot. Plenty of cows, too, which looked up from grazing as we passed by. It was people that were sparse. The farmhouses were half a mile apart and sometimes farther. All pretty much the same—veranda across the front, paint peeling off here and there; brown barn and a couple of sheds out back; with an outhouse and woodpile somewhere in

Me and Billy

between. Sometimes we'd see a woman moving around inside the house or the farmer out back pitching manure out of the barn.

"You know, Possum," Billy said, "we haven't come across anything like a store for a couple of hours. How we going to buy dinner?"

"I didn't think of that," I said. The truth was, I'd kind of been daydreaming about how it would be with the boys running the Home their own way. "There's bound to be a store somewhere. These farmers have got to shop somewhere."

"I don't know. Maybe they grow all their own stuff."

"Let's just keep on. Maybe we'll come to something."

But we didn't. An hour went by and then another hour, close as we could figure. The sun was getting way over in the sky, hanging just above the purple mountains. "I figured we'd of reached those mountains by now," Billy said. "If you was to ask me, I'd say they're farther off from us now than when we started out."

"That can't be, Billy. But they sure don't look any closer."

"I'm mighty hungry," he said. "One way or another I got to get something to eat. Do you reckon that corn's ripe?"

"I doubt it. Not this time of year. Let's stop at the next farmhouse and see if they'll sell us something. They're bound to have milk and eggs, I figure."

On we went. We still hadn't come across a farm-house when we saw a wagon and a mule out in the middle of a hay field. "Must be a farmhouse somewheres around here," Billy said. We picked up our pace, and as we got a little farther along we could see somebody out in the field where the mule and wagon were, swinging a scythe. We went on. When we came abreast of the field, we climbed over the rail fence and started across the mowed stubble. "Looks like a kid," Billy said. We walked on. "Why, it's a girl."

We came up to her. She stopped swinging the scythe and looked at us. It was a girl, all right, about our age, as close as I could judge. She'd got her dress pulled up and tucked into her belt so as to give her legs free play for mowing, and her brown hair was tucked under a straw hat. She was sweating pretty good, and there were bits of seeds and hay dust stuck in the sweat on her face.

Even so, she was mighty pretty. Suddenly I wished I'd cleaned up a little before we climbed over that fence. I reached around back and tucked in my shirt. Billy just stood there staring at her, but I knew more about manners than he did. I sort of bowed. "Howdy, ma'am."

She leaned on the scythe to rest. I figured she'd been at that scything all day, from the amount she'd cut. "Where'd you fellas come from? We don't get a whole lot of strangers out in these parts."

I wasn't about to tell her the exact truth. "From Plunket City. We're heading for the mountains."

"Plunket City? That's twelve miles."

Billy finally caught on that she was pretty and got into the conversation. "We got run out of there," he said. That was exactly what I didn't want him to say, and I gave him a quick knock on his arm. But he was proud of it. "We were working with a fella skinning folks with this elixir, and somebody took a shot at him."

"Blame you, Billy," I whispered.

He grinned. "We had to run for it. We don't know if the fella's dead or just wounded."

"They shot him?" she said. "What on earth for?" She stopped short. "Oh, glory, my skirt." She blushed all pink under the hay dust, which only made her look prettier, and jerked her skirt from under her belt. "Pa'd kill me if he knew some boys saw me like that." She took off her hat, and her hair fell down to the middle of her back. With her fingers, she combed it out a little. Then she took a handkerchief out of the pocket of her skirt and wiped the sweat and hay dust off her face.

I decided I was going to fix Billy's wagon for him. "Don't mind what Billy says, ma'am. He can't always help himself."

Billy grinned. "Possum's right. You can't trust anything about me."

She looked at me. "Is your name really Possum?"

I was glad she asked me instead of Billy, but I wished she'd lighted on a different subject. "Yes," I said. I changed the subject. "How far do you reckon it is to those mountains?"

"How'd you get a name like that?"

But before I could think of what to say, Billy told her. "When they first brought him to the Home, he was curled up in a basket like a possum, so they called him that."

"I'll get you, Billy," I whispered.

"The Home?"

I could see that Billy had made up his mind to make a nuisance of himself, and I figured I'd better take over as much as I could. "The Deacon Smith Home for Waifs," I said. "You have to be pretty smart to go there." I blushed and cursed myself for blushing. I just couldn't get the hang of lying. "Well, maybe that's putting it too strong."

"It's for kids whose pa and ma don't want them," Billy said.

"Glory," she said, shifting her attention to Billy. "You mean your ma and pa didn't want you?"

"You don't know if they didn't want us, Billy. They could have died. Or were just too poor to feed us and figured we were better off in the Home, where we'd eat regular. Maybe the tears were running down their face like a faucet when they took us to the Home."

"Then how come they never came to visit us?" Billy said, giving me a look.

"Maybe they had to move away because they were too poor to live there anymore," I said. "Let's get off this subject." I didn't mind if Billy talked to her some, but I was the one who started talking to her. "Now we told you our names, you got to tell us yours."

"Betty Ann Singletary," she said. "Listen, fellas, I got to get this hay in before dark."

"How come you got to do it by yourself?" Billy said.

"There's just me. The mule kicked Pa and busted his leg. He's better, but not good enough to swing a scythe."

"What about your ma?" Billy said.

I had a feeling he shouldn't have asked that question, and I was right. Betty Ann looked down at the ground. Then she looked back up at us. "Ma's not up to it," she said.

I started to change the subject. "Maybe we could help—"

But Billy busted in. "What's wrong with her?" he said.

Betty Ann looked Billy smack in the eye. "She's just not up to it."

I tried again. "Listen, Betty Ann, if we help you get the hay in, would you sell us some eggs and such?"

She looked at me, so's to shut Billy off. "Pa'd never let you pay for a meal. But I'd be real glad of the help."

"That mule wouldn't of kicked me," Billy said. "The Professor always said, 'Billy, you manage them mules like you was born to it.'"

"Except when you're poking yourself in the eye with the whip handle," I said.

He gave me a quick look, then back to Betty Ann. "You'll see, Betty Ann."

He didn't say anything further, and we started pitching the hay into the wagon. Being as we were town boys, we didn't have any real knack for farm-work, but we'd cleaned out the stable at the Home often enough and knew how to handle a pitchfork. We got the job done. I climbed up onto the pile of hay in the wagon, but Billy got onto the driver's seat and picked up the reins. "You just set there and rest, Betty Ann. I'll drive the mules. Which way is home?"

She didn't climb up but stood there holding the pitchfork, frowning. "I doubt if they'll do what you tell them. The only ones they'll obey are me and Pa."

"Don't you worry," Billy said. "I got a way with mules." She shook her head, but she climbed up onto the wagon beside Billy. He snapped the reins. "Gee up." The mules turned away like they'd seen enough, dropped their heads down, and began to chew at the stubble. "Gee up, I said." The mules didn't pay him any attention but went on chewing. I couldn't see Betty Ann's face from where I sat on the hay pile, but I could tell that she'd got her hand over her mouth. Billy shot her a look. "These are just about the dumbest mules I ever did see." He snapped the reins again. "Blame you, gee up."

Betty Ann couldn't help herself and began to giggle. "I told you," she said.

Billy gave her another look. He knew he was beat, but he wasn't ready to give in. He snapped the reins three or four times and shouted, "Gee up you blame idiots."

Betty Ann laughed out loud. "Billy, you better let me have those reins. Otherwise we'll miss supper and breakfast, too, like as not."

Chapter Ten

The farmhouse was about a half mile away, around a bend in the road. The house was a little more spruce than some of the others. The paint wasn't wore off quite so bad, the roof looked like it had been patched recent, and hanging from one of the big maple trees around the house was a swing, where I figured Betty Ann had swung when she was little and maybe still did.

But they weren't rich, either. The barn had never seen a lick of paint, and one of the front windows had a square of wood in it instead of glass.

We swung around back. Me and Billy pitched the hay up into the barn loft, while Betty Ann unhitched the mules and curried them. While we was working, I noticed a fella with a crutch under one arm and his leg tied up in slats have a look out the kitchen door at us from time to time. He didn't say anything, just looked.

Then we were done, and Betty Ann led us to the house. The man opened the door for us. "Who you got there, Betty Ann?" he said in a quiet voice, kind of firm, but not sore at seeing us there.

"A couple of fellas from Plunket City. They ran away from an orphan home and shot somebody."

"We didn't shoot anybody," I said quickly. "We got shot at."

"Somebody got shot, anyway. They're mighty hungry. They said they'd help me load the hay if we fed them."

"We'll pay for it," I said. "We got a pile of dough." I took the bills out of my pocket and held them out where they could see them.

The man smiled. "You won't pay for a meal in my house," he said. "You just clean up at the pump in the yard, and I'll carve up a few more spuds."

So we washed at the pump, dried ourselves off with a piece of burlap that was hanging on the pump handle, and went on in. It was a nice place—homey, I guess you'd call it. Neat and tidy and done up nice. There were a couple of cloth samplers on the wall with mottoes embroidered into them—"God Bless This House," stuff like that. In the kitchen window there was a jelly jar full of wildflowers. While the potatoes were frying, and sending up just the most handsome smell, Betty Ann took us out to the parlor. In a corner there was a little whatnot cabinet with curios on it—a couple of Indian arrowheads, a bird's nest with speckled eggs in it, a piece of crystal that made rainbow colors when you held it up to the light, and some curled-up seashells. There was a horsehair sofa that seemed better suited for display than sitting on, and across the room a little pump organ with a music book on it opened to "The Letter That Never Came."

"Can you play that organ, Betty Ann?" Billy said.

"Some. Ma was teaching me before . . . before. She could play real good. She used to play for the church choir before she married Pa."

Where was Betty Ann's ma? Was she upstairs sick in bed? What was wrong with her? I was curious, but I knew better than to say anything.

But naturally Billy didn't. "What's the matter—"

I leaped in. "Those potatoes smell powerful good to me. I could eat a bushel of them."

Luckily, just at that minute, Betty Ann's pa called us into the kitchen. We sat down at the old wooden kitchen table, scrubbed so bare it was almost white. Whatever was wrong with Mrs. Singletary, she wasn't eating with us, for there were just four plates on the table. I nudged Billy. "Eat nice," I whispered. "Not like you're shoveling coal into a furnace." Back at the Home, Deacon's sister was always on us about our table manners, the main result being that the boys wouldn't be caught dead eating nice unless she was staring right at them. I wasn't any better than the rest, but now I wished I'd paid more attention to how you were supposed to hold your fork and how to cut your meat.

But good manners or not, considering how hungry we were, it'd be hard to go slow on those potatoes and pork. I was just about to dig in when Mr. Singletary said, "Boys, in this house we always thank the Lord for putting another meal in front of us."

It didn't seem to me the Lord had put those fried potatoes in front of us; we'd worked blame hard in that hay field for them. Still, I dropped my fork, put my hands together, bent my head down, and closed my eyes so I couldn't see those potatoes and that slab of pork in front of me.

"Dear Lord, we heartily thank Thee for what we are about to receive of Thy bounty," Mr. Singletary began. He carried on for a while like that. I couldn't see those potatoes, but with my head bent over like that my nose was only about a foot away from them, and I could smell them, hot and sweet. Then, next door to me, I heard a kind of rustle. I slid one eye open and took a quick look. Betty Ann and her pa had their heads down, praying. Billy had his head down and his eyes closed, too, but his jaw was moving.

Finally Mr. Singletary decided we'd suffered enough and said, "Amen." We dug in. I stuck to my manners, but there was no hope of Billy doing it. Whenever he figured Betty Ann and her pa weren't noticing, he snatched at the food with his fingers.

Betty Ann's pa spent the time asking us a whole lot of questions, and that slowed us down some. And he started right off with the one I always hated. "That's your real name? Possum?"

"Yes, sir."

"What's your last name?"

Here it came again. "That's it. Possum's my whole name."

He frowned. "They never gave you a last name? That wasn't a Christian thing to do."

"I guess they could have given me a last name, but Deacon, I think he figured it served me right for being an orphan."

"Possum, why didn't you give yourself a last name?" Betty Ann said.

"There wasn't any point to it. Nobody would have called me by it. The boys would have just pestered me about it. You know, if I called myself Jones they'd of called me 'bones,' or 'groans,' or something."

"Poor Possum," Betty Ann said, reaching over to pat my arm. That was the first time in my whole life I'd found any advantage in not having a last name. "Well, you're not in the Home anymore. You can give yourself a last name now. Nobody'll ever know it isn't real."

"It wouldn't be the same. I never figured it would count unless I got it done official."

"Oh, I don't know about that, Possum," Mr. Singletary said. "In this country people are forever giving themselves last names. You take somebody just come over from Poland or Italy or someplace, got a name nobody over here can say. Probowinosky or something. Change it to Powell or Porter or something. Happens all the time."

"You mean I could just give myself a name and everybody would have to call me by it?" I couldn't believe it could be true.

"Well, it'd be better if you went to court and got the judge to OK it. That way nobody could argue with you about it. But most people, they don't bother going to court. Just take whatever name suits them."

I sat there feeling excited and happy. I could really give myself a last name if I wanted. I decided not to get in any hurry about it. Choosing a last name was something you ought to think about and do real careful. You wanted to pick one you could stick with for a while.

But I didn't want to say any of this, so I changed the subject. "We were trying to figure how far it was over to those mountains. When we started out we reckoned it was maybe ten miles, but they kept backing off from us."

"Ten miles?" Mr. Singletary said. "More like fifty."

"Fifty miles?" My heart sank. That was a powerful piece of walking. "How long do you reckon it'll take us?"

"Oh, three, four days, most likely." He gave us a look. "Why do you want to go up there?"

Billy gave me a kick under the table. I didn't like lying to them, not with them being so nice to us and all, but I figured I better duck around it as best as I could. "We heard there was a lot of interesting sights up there."

He looked serious and gave his head a shake. "People around here shy away from those mountains. You hear all kinds of stories about fellas going in there and never coming out again. They say you can get lost real easy. My advice is to keep away from there."

"If people never come back," Billy said, "how come they know what it's like?"

"Well, I guess they don't all get lost. Every once in a while a fella comes staggering out near starved to death, all bit and scratched up. He'll tell you how he came up a ravine ten feet ahead of the others, and suddenly they weren't there anymore and are probably dead." He shook his head. "I'd keep out of there."

"Why do they keep going in, if it's so risky?"

"Oh, there's all kinds of stories about what's up there. Rubies as big as your fist lying on the ground, diamonds and gold just for the taking. You can't put any stock in it."

So there wasn't any secret about it. Why shouldn't we put any stock in it? I didn't want to hear that. I didn't say anything.

"That's what we heard," Billy said. "That there was a lake up there with chunks of gold lying all over bottom."

I wished he hadn't said that, but it was too late.

"Who told you that?" Mr. Singletary said.

"The cook back there at the Home," Billy said.

"Where'd he get his information from?"

I jumped in. "He was up there. He saw it himself."

I noticed Betty Ann was staying out of the conversation. In fact, she got up from the table, went over to the stove, and started fixing a plate of food. But I was worrying more about what Pa Singletary was saying about that lake, for I didn't want anyone to take the idea away from me. "No, he saw it himself. He got lost, like you said people did, and stumbled on it. He couldn't swim and couldn't dive down for the gold, so he left, and came back a little while later with a rake to scoop the gold off the bottom. But this time he couldn't find the lake."

Mr. Singletary studied me for a minute. "Do you really believe that story, Possum? You look smarter than that."

I blushed. Still, why couldn't it be true? "Cook said he saw it. He said he saw all that gold on the bottom, plain as day."

"Doesn't it seem odd to you that he couldn't find it again? It's mighty hard to lose a lake."

"Mr. Singletary, you said yourself anybody could get lost up there."

He turned to Billy. "What about you, Billy?"

"I never believed a word Cook said. But he's too dumb to have made that story up."

"So you're just as set on going as Possum is?"

"My heart won't be broke if we don't find that lake. But I reckon it's worth the risk."

I was bound and determined not to get talked out of it, so I changed the subject. "Betty Ann, do you know how to swim?"

"Sure," she said. She had the plate of food on a stool by the stove and was carefully cutting the meat into bite-sized pieces. "There's a swimming hole down the road a ways where a creek goes under a bridge. Sometimes when it's real hot, the kids from the farms around here go swimming there."

I looked at Mr. Singletary and back at Betty Ann. "Suppose we were to stay and help you get the hay in. Would you teach us to swim?"

"I can already swim," Billy said.

"No, you can't, Billy," I said. "You never swam a stroke in your life."

"Oh, yes I did. I swam in that lake once when those Charity Ladies took us out. I was doing pretty good until I sucked in that loose water."

I decided to let it go and looked at Betty Ann and her pa. "It'll take Betty Ann a couple of weeks to get that hay in by herself."

Mr. Singletary nodded, thinking about it. "We could use the help, no doubt of that. But if you're learning to swim just so you can dive down after that gold, I don't think I ought to encourage it."

"Please, Pa," Betty Ann said. "Let them stay."

"I'll sleep on it," he said. He reached into his pocket and pulled out a small gold watch. It wasn't near as noble as the watch that fella Robinson waved around;

even at a distance I could see that some of the gold was wore off. He took out his handkerchief and gave the watch a little polishing. Then he snapped it shut. "Betty Ann, you better get that supper up to your ma. The boys and I'll clean up here." She went off with the plate, but not before I noticed that lying across the food was a big spoon—no fork, no knife.

We cleaned up, and after a bit Betty Ann came down. Pa Singletary took another look at the watch, once again gave it a little swipe with his handkerchief, and closed it. "Time for prayers," he said.

We all knelt down on the kitchen floor, and Pa Singletary prayed. He went on for a good while and only stopped when he realized that Betty Ann was sound asleep setting on her knees. The poor thing, she'd been out in that hay field since first thing in the morning.

Pa Singletary showed us to a little room upstairs. We'd be squeezed, but after sleeping under that van for two weeks, it looked mighty fine. So we lay down, and we were just dozing off when there came through the dark a kind of steady, low moan, like a hum with a gurgle in it. We both sat bolt upright. "What's that?" Billy whispered.

The moan went on and on. "I don't know," I said. "Maybe it's Betty Ann's ma."

"Do you think she's a lunatic?"

The moaning went on. "I don't know," I said. "Maybe that's the problem. Did you notice Betty Ann didn't bring her a knife or a fork, just a spoon? I guess they figure she's dangerous."

Billy flung back the blankets. "I'm gonna look. I never saw a lunatic before."

I grabbed his arm. "It's none of your business, Billy. You stay put."

"I can if I want to," he said. Just then the moaning stopped.

"Besides, she's bound to be locked in. You couldn't get in there, anyway."

Billy lay down again. "I'm going to find out tomorrow. I want to see what she looks like."

There were some things you just couldn't get across to Billy, such as how other people might feel about something. "She probably doesn't look like anything, Billy. Just some lady who moans. Leave her be."

"I want to see what she looks like."

We lay there quiet for a while, and then Billy said, "I don't know about this whole idea, Possum. As soon as I get a look at Betty Ann's ma, I'd rather push off for the mountains."

"We got to learn how to swim sooner or later, Billy. You wouldn't want to be looking down at all that gold and not have any way to get it out, would you?"

"We could learn along the way. There's bound to be streams and lakes here and there."

"Who's going to teach us?" I said.

"I reckon we could figure it out for ourselves."

"Why do that when we got somebody to teach us?"

He didn't say anything for a minute. Then he said, "Possum, I don't know how long I can stand all this praying and having good table manners and watching my mouth because there's a girl around. It doesn't suit me."

"It'll only be a few days, Billy. Just until we get the hay in and learn to swim."

He lay there for a while more. Then he said, "Possum, I know me. It's going to get to me, all this praying and such. I'll only be able to stand it so long. Sooner or later I'm bound to do something bad."

"You can hold out for a few days, Billy. We got to learn to swim."

But I knew all that stuff about learning to swim was a lie. It'd been a lie from the beginning. The truth was, I wanted to stay there for a while. I'd never been in such a place in my whole life. Never been anyplace but the Home, and then camping out by the Professor's van. I wasn't exactly sure what it was about the Singletary place that got me. Neat and tidy, for one. Back at the Home we were supposed to keep ourselves clean and were always being set to scrubbing floors and washing windows. But things didn't hold together too good. There was always clothes laying on the floor, boys hollering and getting into fights, Deacon or somebody yelling, some boy getting a whipping and screaming and crying.

And then Prof skinning people of their hard-earned money and not caring if anybody got better or worse for the medicine. And here was Betty Ann out there in the broiling sun all day getting the hay in, her pa refusing to take any money for supper and giving us a bed to sleep in, where most people would have shoved us out into the barn.

I'd lived so long at the Home, it was hard for me to believe that things could be any different. Could it really be true that people didn't have to fight all the time and try to cheat each other? Billy wouldn't believe it; I knew that. I wasn't even sure I believed it, either. But I wanted to find out more.

So I knew I was lying to Billy when I said we had to stay so's to learn to swim. I didn't feel bad about lying, either.

He didn't say anything for a minute. I lay there listening to him breathe. "Well, I guess if you put it that way, Possum, I got to go along with it. But don't push me too far. I can only take so much praying and tidiness."

I lay there feeling mighty happy. I knew we couldn't stay forever. We weren't invited to, for one thing. For another, I was bound and determined to find that lake. But we could stay for a little while.

Chapter Eleven

Of course Billy couldn't wait until we got out of earshot of Pa Singletary to ask Betty Ann about her ma. We were going along the little farm road toward the hay field, with Betty Ann up on the seat driving the mules, and me and Billy sitting in the wagon.

"Hey, Betty Ann," Billy said. "What's the matter with your ma?"

Betty Ann snapped the reins over the mules. "She's got something wrong with her, is all."

"Leave it alone, Billy," I said in a low voice.

"What makes her moan like that?"

"She only moans sometimes," Betty Ann said.

"She moaned pretty good last night," Billy said. "What happened to her?"

Betty Ann snapped the reins over the mules again but didn't answer. After a while she said, "Going to be mighty hot by ten o'clock. Maybe we should of brought another water jug."

Billy got the idea and dropped the subject. Still, he couldn't let the whole thing rest. At supper time that night he told Betty Ann he'd help carry up her ma's food. Betty Ann said she didn't need any help; it was only a plate and a spoon. And when we were getting ready for bed, he slipped out into the hall and tried the knob on Ma Singletary's door. "Blame thing's locked," he told me when he came back.

"I told you it would be," I said.

"I got to figure how to get in there," he said.

"Forget about it, Billy."

But he didn't. Once I saw him outside the house, studying the windows to Ma Singletary's room. It'd be easy enough to haul a ladder out of the barn and climb up, but he'd have to do it in daylight when he could see in, and Betty Ann or her pa were bound to spot him. Pa Singletary kept the key in his pants pocket, so there wasn't much chance of Billy getting ahold of it. Still, I knew Billy—once his curiosity about a thing got risen up, he couldn't let it rest. To be fair about it, it was hard to let it go, for every couple of nights we'd hear that long, low moan. The sound chilled my blood—I didn't want to see any-one who made a sound like that, but it kept Billy's interest up.

Anyway, we were pretty busy. We'd get up around five-thirty in the morning, milk the cows, take them out to pasture. Around seven we'd sit down to breakfast. Pa Singletary wasn't as fussy about his cooking as Prof, but there wasn't ever any shortage of food—eggs and potatoes, or pancakes and syrup, biscuits and ham, a baked apple with cream so thick you had to plop it on with a spoon, and all the coffee you wanted. We'd stoke up good, for it'd be a long time until lunch.

By that time the dew would be off the hay—you couldn't cut it wet. We'd go on out to the hay field, cut hay, rake it, and load up the wagon. We'd get in a couple of loads in the morning and a couple in the afternoon.

Then, around toward five o'clock, we'd go out to this place where a creek came under a wooden bridge. Betty Ann would climb over the railing and jump in, and Billy would have done it, too, but she wouldn't let him, for she said he didn't swim good enough. Me and Billy would slide in off the bank and paddle around, learning how to keep afloat. None of us had bathing suits: me and Billy swam in our underwear and Betty Ann wore an old housedress. It didn't matter—you'd dry out in twenty minutes in that hot summer sun.

I tell you, it suited me fine. Oh, the work was hard. I'd done hard work at the Home, but it wasn't anything like ten hours a day in a hay field, pitching hay up to the top of a heap on a wagon twelve feet off the ground. But it was nice doing something useful for a change, instead of getting shouted at by Deacon or skinning people with the elixir. We got a lot of fun out of it, telling jokes and stories and teasing each other. Betty Ann was always on Billy about the mules. She'd say, "Say, Billy, I noticed old Nelly staring at you. I shouldn't wonder if she's in love with you. Maybe she wants you to take the reins next load."

Billy'd get even with her by telling her stories about the Home. Billy knew she liked hearing them, and he pitched them higher and higher—how Deacon beat a boy to death, and how the boy's best friend put poison in Deacon's soup, only another boy stole it off the tray and was carted away screaming and was never seen again. "Glory," Betty Ann would say, her eyes wide. "My goodness, I never heard of such a thing."

She liked hearing about Prof and his elixir, too, and Billy'd work up some whoppers there—whole cemeteries worth of dead children and a posse of Pa's that hung Prof from a bridge, only the rope broke and he swam away. That one was from a story in our reading book.

So it went for five or six days. We were getting the hang of swimming—nothing fancy, but good enough so we weren't likely to drown right away. The hay was most nearly in, too, and I knew it wouldn't be much longer before Billy started clamoring to get out of there and off somewhere that he didn't have to use good table manners and pray twice a day. He'd stopped talking about getting a look at Betty Ann's ma, too, and I figured he'd switched his mind to moving on.

I shouldn't have. For real late one night I woke up and realized Billy wasn't in bed beside me. It was dark as could be, clouds over the sky, no moon, no stars. I felt around in the bed. Billy was gone, all right. I swung out of bed and stood up. Right away I saw a thin line of yellow under the bottom of the door. Billy was out there with the candle, sure as anything.

As quick as I could, I slipped the door open. Billy was standing in front of Ma Singletary's door, the candle in one hand, the key in the other. "Billy," I hissed.

He didn't turn his head. He shoved the key into the lock and twisted it. I could hear the click where I stood. I started to tiptoe toward him, but he was too quick for me. Before I could grab him, he slipped the door open and, holding the candle up, poked his head inside. For a moment there was silence. Then came a shriek like nothing I ever heard before—the kind of shriek somebody would give off if they were burning alive. I jumped forward, knocked the candle out of Billy's hand, slammed the door, and locked it. But it was too late, for in half a minute the other doors onto the hall busted open, and there stood Betty Ann and Pa Singletary in their nightshirts, with their own candles.

"What on earth are you boys doing?" Pa Singletary shouted.

"Didn't you hear that scream?" Billy said. "We figured something was wrong." A soft moan came from inside the room.

"Where'd you get that key?"

"It was there, in the door," Billy said.

Pa Singletary looked at me. "Is that right, Possum?" The moaning went on.

"I didn't see it. Billy got there before me." I hated lying to them, but I had to back up Billy. Still, I wasn't about to take the blame for it, either. "Billy sleeps on that side of the bed, and he got out here before me." They could make what they wanted out of that.

Pa Singletary gave Billy a long look. Billy stood his ground. If it had of been me, I'd of blushed and looked down at the floor, up at the ceiling, anywhere but at Pa Singletary. But Billy looked straight back, bold as brass. Finally Pa Singletary said, "All right, you all go back to bed. I'll try to calm her down."

We went back into our room and climbed into bed. I could hear Pa Singletary unlock the door and go in. I waited until I heard the door shut. Then I whispered, "Blame you, Billy, you should never of done that." I felt sick about it, like I'd caused the death of somebody. It wasn't my fault—I'd told Billy often enough to leave it alone. But still, I felt like it was my fault, for I'd brought Billy into their home in the first place. The way I was feeling about him right then, if he'd said something about branching off I probably would have done it.

"Why shouldn't I have done it?" Billy said. "What's so bad about taking a look?"

"It's none of your business. If they wanted us to see her, they'd have shown her to us."

"Why are you getting mad at me, Possum? There wasn't any harm in taking a look."

"No harm? In the first place, how'd you get that key?"

"There wasn't anything to it," he said. "I figured sooner or later someone would leave it lying around. I kept watching for my chance. Sure enough, tonight when Betty Ann came down from bringing her ma her supper—Pa Singletary was out in the barn— she left the key on the table for him. I slipped it in my pocket. I figured Pa Singletary would think Betty Ann still had it."

It was hard for me to understand why Billy couldn't see anything wrong with it. Why didn't it bother him that other people's feelings was hurt? Back at the Home that never mattered, because it was mainly the Deacon and his sister that Billy went after, and they deserved to get their feelings hurt. But here on the outside there were people who didn't deserve it. Billy just couldn't get ahold of the idea that other people counted besides himself. It was useless to argue with him, so I lay there trying to calm myself down and get back to sleep.

I was almost dozing off, when he said, "Possum, don't you want to know what she looked like?"

The truth was, I did. I was curious myself about what a lunatic looked like. But I couldn't admit it, not after telling him he should of kept a grip on himself. "No," I said. "I don't want to know."

"Yes, you do, Possum. Don't give me that."

"No, I don't."

"Yes, you do. Anyway, I'm going to tell you."

I knew I ought to put my hands over my ears and say I didn't want to hear anything about it, but I didn't—I just lay there.

"I knew you wanted to," he said finally. "Well, I only had one quick look before she hollered, but she was a sight. She was dressed up real nice, in a pretty gown with beads or something down the front, a string of pearls around her neck—"

"Real pearls?"

"I don't know. They looked like pearls. And a veil over her head. I know why, too."

"Why?"

"It looked like part of her head was missing."

I sat up. "What?"

"I couldn't see too good. It all happened so fast. If you wouldn't of dunked out my candle, I'd of got a better look. But it seemed like she only had one eye and half an ear on the side where the missing eye was. It looked like a chunk of her head was gone."

"Are you sure? Are you sure it wasn't just a shadow?"

"I'm pretty sure."

"What do you think happened to her?"

"It could have been anything—kicked by a mule, ax head flew off when she was chopping kindling. It could have been anything."

I thought about it for a minute, feeling kind of sick about it.

"Were you scared when you saw it?"

"It kind of took me back. I wasn't expecting it—those fancy clothes, and then a piece of her head tore off."

Now I wished I didn't know about it. The picture of somebody with a chunk gone out of her head kept coming into my mind. That was always the way: you get curious about something and can't rest until you find out about it, and then you're sorry. But of course if you wouldn't have found out, you'd still be curious. There wasn't any way to win in a thing like that. "Poor Betty Ann. It must be awful for her to see her own ma like that every day."

"I reckon she's used to it by now," Billy said.

It took me a long while to get to sleep. I kept thinking that right through the wall next to my head a lady was sitting there in fancy clothes with a chunk gone out of her head. I knew we would have to leave as soon as we got the rest of the hay in. Billy was bound to get curious about her again, and there'd be no telling what he'd do then.

The next day Billy waltzed around like nothing'd happened—it didn't bother him a bit. If it had of been me, I wouldn't have been able to look Betty Ann or her pa in the face for a week. But Billy just chattered away about whether it would rain before we finished getting the hay in and how good he was getting at swimming. I didn't see how he could do it, but he did.

Betty Ann didn't say anything about it and neither did her pa. But they were kind of quiet—didn't say much during breakfast, and out in the hayfield Betty Ann didn't pull any of her usual jokes on Billy about the mules. She just tended to business. Once, when she was at the other side of the field from us, Billy said, "What's got into Betty Ann?"

"You ought to know," I said.

"Aw, come on, Possum. There wasn't any harm in taking a look."

"I don't think Betty Ann agrees with that," I said. It finally got through to him, and he was quiet himself the rest of the day.

It was Pa Singletary who finally brought it up. We were all pretty quiet over supper, just talking a little about how if the rain held off for a couple more days we'd have the hay finished up and about what a good sign it was that there were a lot of crows around, for that meant there'd be a good crop of corn. We'd finished up and were sitting there, resting, when suddenly Pa Singletary said, "Well boys, since you got some idea about Betty Ann's ma, I figured I'd better tell you the rest."

He looked at us. I felt bad about it. "You don't have to tell us if you don't want, Mr. Singletary."

"No, I don't," he said. "But I figured it might do you some good to know."

I looked over at Betty Ann. She had her hands in her lap and was staring down at them. She didn't look up at me, didn't say anything.

"You see," Pa Singletary said, "I know about those mountains, for I went up there myself. I heard all those same stories you were told—rubies as big as your fist, chunks of gold, heaps of diamonds, all just lying around where you could scoop them up for the asking. There were all kinds of stories about how the stuff came to be up there. The one most people favored was that when the conquistadors started fighting the Aztecs down in Mexico and Montezuma got killed, some Aztec priests ran off with bushels of gold and jewels. They came up north to get away and landed up in the mountains, where they figured they'd be safe. But, like the way it happened with a lot of Indians, they caught some disease from the white people and died off like flies. One by one they died out, until there wasn't but one old man left, maybe a hundred years old or something. He knew he was going to die soon and that'd be the end of his tribe. He saw that it was the gold and jewels that did it—if the Aztecs had stayed home, they wouldn't have taken sick the way they did. So he took all the stuff and flung it all around—in the meadows, the woods, the lakes, off mountain ledges, so nobody would ever get tempted by it again. And the stuff is still up there. That's the story most people favored." He stopped and sat there, remembering.

"Do you believe it, Mr. Singletary?" I said.

"I do," Billy said. "What's wrong with it?"

"Oh, there's a lot wrong with it, Billy," Pa Singletary said. "I went into Plunket City and spent a couple of days at the library there studying up on the Aztecs. That story didn't fit in with the facts. There was nothing in the history books about any priests escaping with anything. In fact, it didn't seem like anybody escaped, not to come way up here, anyway. But still, every once in a while you'd hear about somebody coming out of the mountains with a chunk of gold. No diamonds or rubies or emeralds. Just gold. But that was enough for me." He sat still, frowning and remembering.

"You know, people can most generally manage to believe what they want to believe, no matter how strong the evidence is against it. It's just amazing what you can believe if you set your mind to it. I wasn't any different. I went to work on that story, paring it down bit by bit until I got it to where it was believable. Maybe it wasn't a whole passel of priests, but just one who ran off with a knapsack full of gold. That way you didn't need an epidemic to kill anybody off. He could have just got lost up there and starved or got killed by something—a rattlesnake, bear, pack of wolves. You didn't need the part about the priest scattering the stuff around so it wouldn't harm anyone. All you needed was for an animal to smell meat in the knapsack and rip it open. A bear could do that. A wolf could do it. After that, in the nature of things, the stuff would get pretty well scattered—picked up by crows, kicked around by animals, washed into streams by heavy rains."

"So it could of happened," I said.

Pa Singletary shook his head. "It was an easier story to believe, is all. There wasn't any more evidence for it than there was for any other story. It was just more believable."

"What about all those chunks of gold you said people were always finding up there?" I said.

"Hold up there, Possum. You didn't listen to what I said. In the first place, I didn't say anything about *always*. I said *every once in a while*. Every five years, ten years, maybe."

"But still," I said, "that's evidence."

He waggled his finger at me. "You got to listen, Possum. What I said was that every once in a while you'd *hear* about somebody coming out of there with a chunk of gold. Most usually the fellow who told you about it was somebody who'd heard it from the brother of a fellow who was on the most intimate terms with the sister of the wife of the fellow who actually found it. Only he didn't have the chunk of gold anymore, because he lost it in a poker game."

"That proves it," I said. "That's exactly what Cook said—the fella he met lost his gold in a poker game."

Pa Singletary chuckled, but it was a pretty dry chuckle without much cheerfulness in it. "It doesn't prove a thing, Possum, except that when people stumble across a useful story, they like to hang on to it. That's the way it was with me. It's believable that the fellow would lose his chunk of gold in a poker game.

By that time I'd been farming for twenty-five years, since I was a little boy, and my pa before me and my grandpa before him. I was mighty tired of it. I wanted something else for myself. So I worked on that story until I had it ready to try on Betty Ann's ma.

"Well, she had a good deal more sense than me. She kept it in mind that it could have happened, but she also kept it in mind that a lot of other things not nearly as interesting could have happened, too. Such as that there never were any Aztecs with bushels of gold anywhere near these mountains, and if over twenty or thirty years a couple of fellas found two or three pebbles of gold in those mountains, there wasn't anything unusual in that.

"But she saw I had got my heart set on going up there. She knew me. She knew I was getting more and more restless—always talking about some scheme to get off the farm. Go into Plunket City and set up this or that business, take up surveying, anything but farming. So she told me once we got the corn in and things generally buttoned down for the fall, she could handle the farm for a few weeks. Betty Ann was six, old enough to be helpful. So I went. There's a little town at the foot of the mountains called Wasted Gulch that's kind of a jumping-off place for the mountains. Folks up there have seen an awful lot of people pass through there, planning on being rich. I didn't have to tell anyone what I was there for. There wasn't any other reason for visiting Wasted Gulch. Nobody said anything about it.

"So I got me a little tent, food, blankets, and such, and went up into those mountains. I was up there three weeks. I searched everywhere, in streams, gullies, places where it looked like the rain had washed through. I didn't find anything—not a single thing. Finally I ran out of food and came down out of there, looking the way most people look when they came down—covered with bites and scratches, half starved, my clothes torn and filthy, and sort of crazy from having been alone all that time."

"Is it true about getting lost?" I said.

"Yes, that's true. There's no magic to it. Those mountains are pretty rugged—sharp peaks, cliffs, gullies that fold back on themselves. I was always coming around a corner to find myself up against a mountain wall or a drop-off too steep to climb down. I'd turn around to go back and, like as not, get confused and couldn't find the way I got up there."

"How'd you get out?" Billy said.

"There's an old rule: find a stream. It'll always go downhill and lead you into a bigger stream. Sooner or later you'll come out. But I was pretty well lost for a while.

"Well, I got back to Wasted Gulch and rested there in the little hotel they got for a couple of days before setting out for home. None of the regulars up there said anything to me about the mountains one way or another—just passed the time of day in a polite way. But there was a fellow there hanging around the lobby of that hotel who was looking to go up into the mountains himself. He asked me if I'd found anything. I didn't lie to him. But I knew I'd made a fool of myself, and I didn't want to admit it. So I gave him a wink. Now, I wasn't fooling any of the regulars—they knew well enough why I was winking. But this other fellow, he believed in that wink, for he wanted to. And when I took off for home, he followed my trail. I wasn't back here more than ten minutes, sitting there with Betty Ann on my lap, telling my story and feeling mighty glad to be home, when this fellow busted through the door waving a pistol. What'd I find up there, exactly where was it, and such.

"I was stuck. I told him I hadn't found anything, it was all just a wink, but naturally he thought I was holding out on him and didn't believe me. He stuck the pistol to Betty Ann's head and said he'd kill her first, and if I still didn't tell he'd kill Ma. I pointed across to the windowsill there and said, 'There's the gold, right there.' He took his eyes off Betty Ann just for a second. I shoved Betty Ann onto the floor and grabbed the fellow's arm, trying to twist that pistol out of it. It went off." He stopped, for he was breathing pretty hard. "I guess you know where the bullet struck."

We sat there dead still. For the longest time Mr. Singletary sat looking out the window. I could hear him breathe. He'd been living with that in his mind for all these years and would go on living with it for years to come, for how could he ever forget it when

136

every day he had to unlock that room and look at that face with the chunk shot off it?

All that silence was making Billy nervous and fidgety. "What happened to the fella who shot her?"

Pa Singletary raised his head up. "When he saw what he'd done, he lost his stomach for it and ran. I never knew what happened to him. I doubt that he tried to go up into the mountains, though." Then he took out his gold watch and flipped the cover open. "Time for prayers," he said.

Chapter Twelve

I knew that Pa Singletary had told us that story for our own good. Well, told it for my own good, anyway, for I didn't suppose that he cared much about Billy's good right then, although he was such a nice fella, he might have. But I wasn't going to let it throw me. I hadn't heard that stuff about the Aztecs before, but it made pretty good sense. How else could that gold have got up there? Sure, Pa Singletary had had some hard luck out of the whole thing, but that didn't mean it would be hard luck for everybody. Somebody was bound to have good luck—that stood to reason.

Oh, I would like to have stayed for a while longer. Living at the Singletarys' was almost like paradise, if you discounted the hard work. It was still kind of unbelievable to me that people could go along being nice to each other day after day without ever getting tired of it. I figured it had to do with what had happened to Ma Singletary: they'd got enough woe for themselves and didn't need to add to it.

But as much as I liked being at the Singletarys', I knew I had to get Billy out of there. He was going to do something to them, sooner or later. It wouldn't be fair to them. And to be honest, I had a hankering to find that lake full of gold and fix myself up with a last name. Maybe after I'd got some gold I'd come back here, buy Pa Singletary a gold watch chain for his watch, take Betty Ann for a trip over to Plunket City, and buy her some dresses—the ones she had were patched pretty fair.

Of course we didn't talk about the gold lake in front of Pa Singletary; even Billy could see we oughtn't to do that. But we talked about it when we were haying, and after a while Betty Ann got curious herself. "You boys really going to do it? After what Pa told you?"

"Sure we are," I said. "Your pa didn't know about that lake. All the gold washed into there."

She sighed. "I wish I could go on an adventure. I wish I could go anywhere. I hardly ever get off the farm. Down to the church on Sundays, over to Plunket City maybe once a year for clothes and such. I've never seen the ocean, never seen the mountains except from a distance. You boys are always having adventures—getting shot at for skinning people, going into the mountains hunting for gold. I wish I could go on an adventure."

"Why don't you come with us, Betty Ann?" Billy said. "Just run off with us."

She looked down at the ground, thinking, and then she looked up at Billy. "I couldn't do it," she said. "It wouldn't be right."

"What's wrong with it?" Billy said.

"It'd break Pa's heart. I'm all he's got now."

"That's his lookout," Billy said. "Besides, it was his own fault."

She shook her head. "I thought about it a lot, Billy. Thought about being stuck on the farm, never seeing the ocean, never having adventures. I just never could twist it around to where it would be right for me to leave. You got to figure things like that out for yourself, and however it comes out, you got to do it."

"Not me," Billy said.

"How could I leave? Pa can't look after Ma and manage the farm himself."

"Maybe your ma will die soon," Billy said.

"Billy," I said, "haven't you got any blame sense at all? Don't say things like that."

"Maybe she will," he said.

"I don't want her to die, Billy," Betty Ann said. "I've got used to the way she is. It's like having a puppy—you've got to love it even though it's always wetting the rug and chewing up your slippers. Ma can't help herself any more than a puppy can."

She didn't seem to mind talking about it, so I said, "What was she like before?"

140

"Oh, she was always looking on the cheerful side of things. When something went wrong, she'd say, 'Betty Ann, just look on the bright side.' She'd say, 'No use crying over spilt milk, you have to take the bad with the good.'" She shook her head. "I don't reckon she figured how bad it was going to be."

"If it was me," Billy said, "I'd rather of taken that bullet straight between my eyes and got it over with."

"Billy, will you plea—" I started.

But Betty Ann cut in. "That's what Pa says. He says if Ma knew what would become of her, she'd rather have died. Sometimes I see him looking at her when she's acting real strange, and I know he's thinking how awful she'd feel if she could come back to her old self and see what she was. I kind of figure he's thought of putting her out of her troubles. But not me. I can't help loving her—she's like a puppy to me."

"Do you think your pa might do it sometime, Betty Ann?" Billy said. The idea interested him.

She shook her head firmly. "No. He'll think about it, but he won't do it, for it would be a sin before the Lord. He says he owes it to her to make her as happy as he can and hope that in time the Lord will take pity on her. Sooner or later she'll go, he says. But I'll miss her." She sighed again. "Still, I wish I could go on an adventure with you boys."

The truth was, I wished she could, too. I'd got to where I liked her a whole lot, and I wished she could come with us. "Betty Ann, maybe someday you'll get to go yourself. Maybe if we find that lake, we'll come back to get you and take you up there ourselves."

"No," she said. "I couldn't go up to the mountains." Then she brightened. "But maybe we could go somewhere."

"All right. Once we find that gold, we'll come back and take you somewhere."

Finally the day came when it was time to say good-bye. Pa Singletary stoked us up real good at breakfast—eggs and potatoes *and* pancakes and syrup both. "No telling when you boys are likely to get your next good meal," he said. We washed up the dishes, and then Pa Singletary shook our hands, and Betty Ann gave us each a nice big hug. I near busted out crying when she did that, and when we finally started for the door, I could see she was holding off the tears, too. But then the door shut behind us and we were off. I kept looking back over my shoulder at the little farmhouse, hoping I'd see something in one of the windows, and after a bit I saw a curtain jump and something move behind the glass. Then we were around the bend and gone. But for the next while I kept thinking about those people—how around this time Betty Ann was probably milking the cows and Pa Singletary was fetching breakfast upstairs to Betty Ann's ma.

We went along for a couple days, hitching rides on farm wagons when we could and walking the rest of the time. From time to time we'd hit a village where we could stock up on ham, cheese, bread—stuff we could eat raw. Neither of us was much of a hand for cooking. For the first day or so those mountains kept walking backward away from us; but at the end of the second day we realized that they were sticking much farther up into the sky than before, and the color had turned from hazy purple to green and gray—trees and rocks.

"I believe we're catching up to them," Billy said. "It won't be long now." I was getting excited. It had been a long time, and we'd come a long way, but now the real thing was about to start.

On we went, and by and by we came to an old wooden sign saying WASTED GULCH. The paint was mostly worn off, but it was clear enough. There wasn't much need of it, anyway, for there wasn't anything else around there that needed a name. A half hour later we began to make out the town down the road—the usual old wooden buildings sagging in four or five different directions. Like most of these places, there wasn't much more to it than a quarter mile of one- and two-story buildings—anything three stories high stood out like a monument.

Shortly we came into town. Now we could see it wasn't quite the usual thing: it was worse. There was hardly any paint on anything at all, just gray wood everywhere and most of the buildings likely to fall in on themselves if you gave them a hard look. There was a general store, barbershop, two or three saloons, and a few other stores. The center of things seemed to be Wilson's Miners' Supply, and the Majestic Hotel, which was majestic in the sense that it was three stories tall but was otherwise as gray and sagging as the rest of the town. A couple of loafers leaned against the front of the miners' supply, and three or four sat in rocking chairs on the Majestic Hotel veranda, chewing straw. That was about it, except for the mountains looming over it all.

"Mighty lively place, isn't it?" Billy said. "I shouldn't wonder if there's some kind of fair going on, from all the excitement around."

"What do you expect they do for a living here?" I said. "Mostly doing business with people going up into the mountains to look for gold, I guess."

We stood there looking around. "What do you want to do, Possum? Let's put up at that hotel. I never stayed in a hotel before."

I wondered what they'd say if a couple of kids walked in asking to be put up. "They might start asking us where our ma and pa were and where we were from. I don't trust what might happen. We better sleep on the ground. Might as well save the money, anyway."

"Well, let's try that general store for some grub," Billy said. "I'm hungry."

We started along the wooden sidewalk, skirting around the snoozing dogs, just ambling along, when suddenly Billy grabbed my arm.

"Look, Possum." He pointed. Tacked up on the side of a building was a familiar handbill:

NOTED PROFESSOR ALBERTO SANTINI, SAVANT
OF THE HEALING ARTS . . .

And it went in the usual way from there.

"See, I told you, Possum. They couldn't kill him. He's too tough." He was pretty excited.

"Wait a minute, Billy. That could be an old poster left over from last year."

Billy went up closer and peered at it. "It's new. It'd be more faded if it was old." He did a couple of little dance steps.

"What date does it say?"

"Just, 'This Sunday.'"

"He could have come and gone. It could have been last week."

"Don't always look on the dark side, Possum. Look on the bright side, like Ma Singletary used to say."

It was the worst luck. Here we'd got to within a half mile of the mountains, and this had to happen. I just couldn't believe it. "Billy, forget about the blamed Prof. He near got us killed the last time, and he's certain to get us in trouble again. You promised."

"Now don't get fired up, Possum. We'll go for the gold lake. I just got to find Prof first to see if he's all right."

"He isn't all right, Billy," I shouted. "He never was all right and he never will be all right. He's a crook."

145

"Now, Possum, calm yourself down. I never saw you all riled up like this."

"Well, I got a right to be riled up. That blame Prof hasn't ever been anything but trouble. So far as that goes, neither have you."

Right away I was sorry I'd said it, for a hurt look went across his face, like I'd hit him. "Possum, you don't mean that."

"I'm sorry," I said. I hated hurting his feelings, even if he deserved it. "I spoke too quick. But blame it, Billy, you'd exasperate a watermelon."

"I promise, Possum, we'll go look for that lake. But just let me see Prof this one time. After that I'll leave it alone."

I didn't trust that for a minute. But I could see where he'd never rest if he didn't at least get a look at Prof. Chances were pretty good that Prof wasn't around—had come and gone a month ago. "All right, Billy. But then we're heading for the mountains."

"We'll find him," Billy said. "He's around here somewheres. I know it. Come on. Let's go ask in that general store. They're bound to know." He trotted off, and I came along after him, trying to figure out a way to talk him out of it, if it turned out the Professor was in town.

We went into the general store. Same as any general store—barrels of molasses, sugar and flour, cheese and bread in a glass cabinet, folded overalls stacked up

146

on the floor, shoes hanging from the wall by the shoe-strings, tins of food on the shelves, shovels and picks in a jumble in a corner. The fella behind the counter was mostly bald but made it up on his face, which hadn't been shaved for five or six days. "What can I do for you boys," he said. "Your pa sent you in for treats?"

"We don't have any pa," Billy said. "We got our own money."

The less anyone knew about us the better, I figured. "How much is that chunk of cheese?"

But before the storekeeper could answer, Billy leaped in. "That fella on the poster out there—the medical professor? Did he give his show yet?"

"Who? The snakebite fella?"

"Snakebite?" Billy said. It was clear that the Professor had switched his game.

"Yup. He had this here stuff he said was good for snakebite." He jerked his chin toward the mountains. "In case you was to go up into the mountains and run into snakes. He said it kept mosquitoes off, too, if you rubbed it on your face. And if you cut yourself you could pour it on and you'd heal overnight."

"Are the snakes bad up there?" I said.

The storekeeper shrugged. "This here professor seemed to think they was."

"What do you think?"

He shrugged again. "I reckon where you got rocks warm from the sun, you'll have snakes."

"Where's he at now?" Billy said.

The storekeeper looked at him. "This here professor? That was a couple of days ago. He didn't sell but two or three bottles of the stuff. I reckon he's moved on to someplace where the pickings is more charitable." He scratched his head. "Mighty popular fella, seems like. There was another fella in here just a little bit ago asking about him, too."

My legs went weak, and my head went cold. "What sort-of-looking fella?" I said, trying to sound like I wasn't much interested.

"Dressed up fancy. Don't see many up here like that. Derby hat, gold watch chain across his coat."

I just wanted to get out of there as fast as possible. "Well, thanks," I said. "We'll just take a loaf of bread and that chunk of cheese and won't bother you further."

He didn't move. "Funny the way so many people is looking for that professor. How do you explain it?"

"To be honest, we don't know this professor. He's Pa's cousin, and he said we was to look him up."

The storekeeper squinted at me. "I thought you said you didn't have no pa."

"He said that," I said, jerking my thumb at Billy. "We're just cousins. I got a pa." I took a dollar out of my pocket, which I figured would interest him. It did. He got us the bread and cheese and a jar of cider, and we skedaddled out of there. We went down an alley until we came to a patch of trees and sat down to eat the bread and cheese, talking all the while.

"We got to find him," Billy said. "We got to warn him that Robinson's around."

"Billy, we oughtn't to get within ten miles of him. Not with Robinson hunting him down."

"Possum, we got to warn him."

"Why? We don't owe him anything. He cheated us on our money as much as he could and near got us shot in the bargain."

"Still," Billy said. "You don't want to see him killed, do you? You're the one always saying if you can help somebody, you got to do it."

I gave that a little thought. "I think maybe I'm changing."

Billy gave me a long look. "How come you're changing all of a sudden? You don't look any different."

I was kind of interested in figuring it out myself. "It wasn't any one thing," I said. "Just everything together. It seems like everybody's got a reason why their troubles is due to somebody else; but when you come down to it, they brought it on themselves. Look at Pa Singletary. Look at Prof."

"Prof just made a mistake, is all, Possum. He meant to tell those folks to take their little girl to a doc, but they got away too fast. I don't see where that was his fault."

"Maybe he shouldn't of been out skinning people in the first place."

He thought for a minute. Then he said, "Even so, Possum, you wouldn't want to see anybody get killed, would you? Especially when you could of saved him."

That was a hard one to get around. Suppose the Professor got shot dead? We'd hear about it for certain, for nobody with a good story like that would rest until he'd told it sixteen or twenty times, and it'd get to us sooner or later. If I let the Professor get shot, I'd have to live with it the rest of my life, the way Pa Singletary had to with Betty Ann's ma. "No, I guess not," I said.

"We'll just go see him for a minute," Billy said. "Just to warn him."

"We don't know where he is, Billy."

"I'll go ask that fella in the general store. He seems to be keeping an eye on things around here."

"I'll go," I said. I didn't trust Billy. If the fella in the store said he didn't know where the Professor was, Billy was likely to come back with some story about how he was over here, or over there, just so's we could run around looking for him.

So I went back to the store, while Billy waited outside to keep a watch out for Robinson. There was another customer in there, a fella taking his time deciding between a green shirt and a blue shirt. I stood there fidgeting from one foot to the next, looking over my shoulder through the window every minute, in case

Robinson should turn up. Finally, just when I was deciding I couldn't take it anymore, the customer said he'd have to think it over and left.

The storekeeper gave me a grumpy look. "I suppose you changed your mind about the cheese and want your money back. Well, you can't have it."

"No, no," I said. "The cheese was perfect. What I wanted to ask, did you have any idea where that snakebite professor might have got off to?"

He shrugged. "If I'd known I'd of told you. In Wasted Gulch most strangers are either heading for the mountains or away from them as fast as they can travel." He scratched his head. "I'll tell you, though. The fella who was looking for him went by the door not five minutes ago. He's striding along right quick. I'd ask him, if I was you."

"Which direction was he going in?"

"Thataway," he said, pointing.

"Thanks," I said, and dashed out of there. "Billy, Robinson just went down the street in a mighty rush. The storekeeper figures he's onto where Prof is."

"We got to save him, Possum. We got to."

Chapter Thirteen

Of course we didn't really have any idea where the Professor might be. As far as that went, we didn't know whether Robinson knew, either, or was just looking around for him the way we were. But Billy had got it figured that since Robinson was walking toward the west, the Professor couldn't be on the east side of town, for Robinson would have spotted him coming in.

"Unless he saw him out there and already shot him," I said.

"Naw, if he did that, he'd of got himself out of town as quick as he could."

So we set off, slipping through town as quick as we could, looking around all the while for Robinson. In ten minutes we'd got out of town and were getting into hilly countryside covered with scrub oaks and low pines.

Here and there we'd come across a piece of pastureland with a few scrawny cows standing around looking miserable, and once we saw in the distance a cabin with a tassel of smoke coming out of the chimney. But mostly it was just the foothills of the mountains.

The road wasn't hardly more than a dusty trail winding along through the trees. The trail began to slant downward, and in a little bit we could see patches of silver through the trees. "There's a creek there," Billy said. "He's camped by it. I guarantee it."

"Maybe," I said.

"How much you want to bet?" Billy said. He began to trot. There was just no holding him back, and I trotted after him. At the bottom of the slope, the road curved to follow along the creek. We came around the bend and, sure enough, parked in among the trees by the side of the road was the van. "I told you, Possum," Billy said.

My heart sank. Plain bad luck again. "What if he wants his twenty-two dollars back?"

"He won't. He was too busy getting shot at to count how much we skinned off him. Besides, we can always say we left it under the van for him when we ran."

"You think he'll believe that?"

"No. He's not that much of a fool. But he can't prove it."

We trotted on, and then we saw him, crouched in front of a little fire, holding a frying pan over the flames. Billy stopped. "Let's surprise him," he said. We slipped into the woods and came along through the trees, going easy. When we were about twenty feet away and could smell the ham and potatoes hot and tasty, we gave a shout: "Hey, Prof."

He came near to dropping the frying pan. He swiveled around, his right hand flashing, and then he was pointing a pistol at us.

My heart jumped. "Don't shoot," I hollered. "It's me and Billy."

"I'll be blowed," he said. He shoved the pistol back into his pants pocket. "Where the devil did you two turn up from?"

"We've been wandering all over the place looking for you," Billy said. "We were desperate to know if you got killed or not."

He jabbed at the ham in the frying pan with his finger to see how it was coming along. "That would have been mighty kind of you if it was true." He pulled out a fried potato and bit off a piece. "But seeing as it ain't likely, I don't know as I ought to feel over grateful."

"It's true," Billy said. "We figured you were out here somewhere. We came to warn you. Robinson's back there in Wasted Gulch asking people if they saw you."

"Robinson? He's here in Wasted Gulch?"

"Yep. Possum found out. He was asking the fella in the general store where you were."

The Professor frowned and shook his head. "Blow it all. Why can't he give it a rest?"

"What're you going to do?"

"Well, I ain't going to budge until I eat my lunch, that's certain." He hunkered down and shoved the frying pan over the flames, shaking it a little to keep the ham from burning.

Billy sniffed the air. "I don't reckon you got a little extra of that ham."

"Same old Billy," the Professor said. "Well, take a look in that van and see if you can find a couple of more spuds." So we got the potatoes, and he cut them into the frying pan. While they were frying, he told us about the shooting, all of us keeping our eyes down the road for the sight of anyone coming along.

"See, there was too many witnesses in that there square. If he'd killed me, they'd of had to put him in jail. Of course he might of got off in the end with that story of his, but he might of got hung, too. So he just winged me in the leg." He reached down and gently touched the calf of his right leg. "It still ain't healed. I'm limping. I'll carry the scar of it to my grave."

"Maybe it's time you got into another business, Prof," I said.

"I ain't gonna let that fella scare me," he said, looking around like he hoped nobody was listening. "I picked up this here little pistol awhile back. Still, I wouldn't like him to get the drop on me when I was alone out in the woods like this. I wouldn't trust what he might do if there wasn't any witnesses around."

As far as I was concerned, the farther away he was from us the better. "Well, he's looking for you."

He squinched up his face so that everything was pulled toward the middle. "Blow it all." He unsquinched his face and gave the pan a shake. "Do you reckon he's got an idea where I am?"

"It didn't seem like it," I said, "or he wouldn't of been asking. But he may have found out by now. It didn't take us long to find you. There isn't but one road out of Wasted Gulch. Maybe you better pack up and move on."

"I hate to always keep running from that fella. It don't set right inside me. Gives me a low opinion of myself." He sighed. "Still, he has all the advantage— spot the van somewhere, sneak up on me at night, and plug me through the window."

"That's what I mean," I said. "It isn't worth taking the chance."

He squinched his face up again. "I wish he'd give it up."

By now the ham and potatoes were sizzling and giving off a fine smell. The Professor dished it out, and we fell to eating—you couldn't hear any sound but lips smacking. When we got done and were sitting there resting, with our backs up against the trees, the Professor said, "What've you been up to, since I last seen you? And don't give me none of that about searching for me night and day." So we told him about the farm and the woman with the chunk gone out of her head. When we finished, he looked down at his hands and back up at us again. "The way I calculate it, I come up twenty-two dollars short after you boys run off and left me getting potted by Robinson. I reckon you figured I wouldn't notice, as I would be dead."

"What?" Billy said. "Didn't you find that money? We left it right under the van before we skedaddled." Quickly he shifted the subject. "You can't blame us for running, Prof. Did you expect us to wait around there until he got done with you and had the leisure to shoot us, too?"

"Getting back to the twenty-two dollars, Billy," the Professor said. "If I was to believe you left twenty-two dollars lying on the ground, they'd lock me up for sure. How much do you reckon you got left?"

"Honest, Prof, we didn't take it. All we got is the three dollars each we earned on that farm."

"I'm ready to believe you only got three dollars left. That part I'll believe." He looked sour and shook his head. "Honest to Pete, you can't trust nobody these days. When I was kid, a man's word was his bond." Suddenly he stood up. "I reckon it's time to move. There ain't any point in sitting here waiting for Robinson to turn up." He looked off through the woods. "I was just thinking. I'm not a hard-hearted fella. I ain't one to carry a grudge. 'Let bygones be bygones' is my motto. I'll tell you what. I'll let you come back to work for me, and we'll forget about paying me back the twenty-two dollars. You can work it off as we go along. I reckon by the end of summer we'll be even."

I jumped in quick. "That's mighty kind of you, Prof, but me and Billy have our hearts set on finding that golden lake before we do anything else."

"Possum, let's not be in a—"

I snatched up the plates. "Come on, Billy, let's go down to the creek and wash our plates."

There was a little stretch of rocky beach along the edge of the water. I knelt down and began to scrub off the tin plates with a handful of sand. "Now listen, Billy, you promised." I turned my head up to look at him. "You got to keep your promise."

"I didn't exactly promise that," he said. "All I promised was if we didn't find him, we'd head for the mountains. I didn't promise what we'd do if we found him."

I couldn't remember exactly what he'd promised. "Well, that's so," I said. "But you knew what I meant. We're supposed to be looking for that lake."

"If we hadn't of stuck around that farm so long, we'd of already found it," he said.

"You wanted to stay until you got a look at Ma Singletary. Right along you agreed we were going after that gold. You can't go off with Prof instead."

He knew I was right, and he stood there struggling to get himself loose of it. "Possum, suppose we don't find that lake? Then we'd of missed a good chance to go off with Prof."

"I don't see what's so good about putting yourself in the way of Robinson."

"Oh, Prof's sure to move to a new territory—"

Then through the woods came a shout. There weren't any words to it, just a sharp, sudden howl. I jumped up, and we stood looking at each other. "Robinson's got the drop on him," Billy whispered. "Sure as we're standing here. We got to save him."

My heart began to race, and I could feel a drop of cold sweat drip down my side under my shirt. All I wanted to do was leap into the creek, swim across, and run off through the woods as fast as I could. "Robinson's going to kill him in five minutes, sure as anything," Billy said.

There wasn't any doubt of that. Robinson had got Prof in the woods off a quiet road. He'd shoot him, drag the body off into the woods where the animals would get him soon enough, and disappear.

Why did it matter to me? The truth was, it didn't. I'd just as soon see the Prof dead where he wouldn't be luring Billy away all the time. But I didn't want to have a dead man on my conscience. I saw what it did to Pa Singletary—ruined his whole life and Betty Ann's, too. "How do you figure to do it, Billy?"

He looked quickly around at the trees, the ground, the creek. "Stones," he said. "Grab up a shirtful. If we

159

get his attention, maybe Prof'll have a chance to go for his gun."

We stripped off our shirts, piled eight or ten stones into them, bundled up the shirts, and started slipping through the woods toward the van as quiet as we could. My arms and legs felt all trembly, and my breath was going fast. One thing was in our favor: we were on the creek side of the van, and they were on the road side of it. We could make out the shape of the van through the woods dead ahead. On we came until we weren't more than twenty yards from it. Now we could hear their voices, but we couldn't make out much of what they were saying.

We stopped. "We got to figure out which way he's facing, so we can come up on him from behind," Billy whispered.

"If we go closer and lay flat on the ground, we can look under the van and see which way his boots are facing," I said.

We slipped forward. Now we could hear their voices better. "The boys," Robinson said. "Where'd they go to, you piece of rubbish?"

"Now be reasonable, Robinson," Prof said, his voice sort of quavery. "You got a Christian duty not to murder people. It says so in the Bible. How you going to face the Lord on Judgment Day with a murder on your soul?"

"I should think you could answer that question for yourself. Where are those two little crooks? I'd just as soon bury them alongside you—spare the world their presence when they're grown up and can do real damage."

There was a little silence. We heard Prof take in a big gulp of air. "How'd you come to find out where I was?"

"Your little crooks. The fellow in the general store told me a couple of boys had been asking about you. I knew at once it was them. I kept my eyes open and, sure enough, I spotted them heading out of town. I just tracked them here. I've been sitting out in the woods for the past half hour, watching you stuff your faces. Where'd those boys go?"

I kind of shuddered: he could of popped us off sitting there with a mouthful of ham and potatoes. I looked at Billy. We didn't dare speak, but I could see a frown flicker across Billy's face. We didn't have any time to worry about it. I dropped to the ground and looked under the van. I could see two pairs of boots. I didn't have any trouble figuring out which were Robinson's— I'd seen the Prof's often enough, sitting on the ground beside him while he snoozed.

"Where are those boys, rubbish?" Robinson said again.

"No need to make insulting remarks," Prof said. "Like as not they saw you coming and have run off to get help. I expect the sheriff'll be along any second now."

"Ha, ha," Robinson said. "Or else they're crouched

in the woods watching the whole thing. No jury would convict me on their testimony." He raised his voice so it would carry through the woods. "Besides, if I catch them out there I'm going to plug them, too."

I didn't doubt that he would. I scrambled to my feet and pointed to show Billy which way Robinson was facing. Without saying a word, we slipped off through the woods, crouching low, circling around maybe fifty feet back from the van. When we got around far enough, we could see them, standing on opposite sides of the little campfire, which was down to embers. Robinson was standing there with both arms out-stretched. In one hand he had his pistol; in the other he had Prof's gun. I went cold, looked at Billy, and pointed. He nodded. We eased the shirtfuls of stones to the ground and picked up two stones apiece. Billy made the shape of "one" with his lips, then "two," and "three," and we let fly, getting our second stones off before the first ones hit. I saw one hit Robinson in the middle of his back and another one his shoulder.

"Hey," he shouted. He started to swivel around but thought better of it. We snatched up more stones and let fly a second round. Robinson made a half turn and, keeping his face toward Prof, stretched his right arm out toward the woods and fired a shot. I near jumped out of my skin. He wasn't likely to hit us firing blind, but it was mighty scary getting shot at, anyway.

"We're not hitting him hard enough, Possum. Let's get closer." He dashed forward ten feet. "Try to hit his head." Robinson fired again, and I heard the leaves over my head whisper. I raced up to Billy, dragging the shirtful of stones, and threw again. This time I actually heard the stone hit his head with a clunk. He staggered and turned toward us. A stone caught him dead in the chest. The pistol went off, and then Prof charged through the campfire, embers flying, and jumped on him. He pitched forward on his face, both guns going off at once. We dropped the stones and ran forward. By the time we got there Robinson had twisted around under the Prof and was lying face upward. Prof was flat on top of him, his arms wrapped tight around Robinson, to keep his arms pinned tight. "Smash him, boys, before he kills us all," Prof shouted. We dove in on the pile, searching for the guns. Then suddenly there came one more shot, this one so loud it seemed to go off in my head. Robinson gave a long, deep sigh, stopped struggling, and lay still.

Slowly we climbed off him, watching him close. He lay still, staring upward. A little splotch of blood on the side of his coat was growing wider. I figured the bullet had gone through his ribs at an angle and hit smack into his heart.

Chapter Fourteen

We dragged Robinson a good ways back into the woods. Prof got a shovel out of the van and set me and Billy to work digging a grave, while he went back to the van and covered up signs of the fight. The sweat was pouring off me like a faucet. It was hot work digging that grave, but that wasn't where all the sweat was coming from. I'd helped to kill a man. It made me feel awful inside, like something was rotting in there. I don't know how that gun went off, and I don't reckon anyone else did, either. But I'd been in on it; there was no way around that. I felt terrible. I wished I was somebody else. Finally I said, "Billy, I can't stand him staring up at the sky like that. Let's turn him over." So we did, but it didn't make me feel much better.

"How deep do you figure we got to go?" Billy said.

"Six feet is what they always say, but I reckon we don't need to go that deep. Just so long as the animals can't smell him and dig him out."

"We'll pile rocks on him. We don't want some dog carrying his arm home to the sheriff."

It took us a good hour to get the hole deep enough to where we figured the animals couldn't smell him. It was the worst hour I ever spent in my life. I'd rather Deacon whip me the whole hour than dig a grave for a fella I helped to kill. I wondered if I'd ever get over it, or if I would go on feeling like this for the rest of my life. I hoped I'd get over it; for if I didn't, I'd have to kill myself, too.

Prof kept coming back to see how we were doing, but he said he had to keep an eye out for people coming along the road and would go away again. He'd got the mules hitched up and was ready to move the minute the body was buried. Finally we got the job done. Prof took the gold watch out of Robinson's coat and a handful of bills out of his pocket. Then we slid the body into the hole, piled on such rocks as we could find, and shoveled in the dirt. In fifteen minutes we had the hole filled in and covered over with leaves and broken branches. Prof looked it all over real careful. Finally he nodded. "That ought to do it," he said. "So long as the animals don't get him, it ain't likely anyone'll be traipsing around here soon. In six months nobody'll be able to recognize him."

165

"Possum," Billy said, "we got to get away from this town for awhile. Once word goes out that Robinson disappeared, they'll be suspicious of us. We better go with Prof."

"Billy, blame you—"

Prof held up his hand. "Boys, I guess I got to rescind that there generous offer I made a while back. It won't do for you fellas to come along with me."

It was clear enough why. Prof saw that back in Wasted Gulch we were connected to Robinson. If anyone ever found Robinson's body, the blame would fall on us, not him. That suited Prof right down to the ground. The last thing he wanted was to have us as partners anymore. If anything about Robinson ever came up, he'd say he was halfway across the state at the time and didn't know anything about it. Like as not he'd throw in something about us having it in for Robinson for some reason. Oh, he'd hang us with it if he could. But it suited me, too, so I said, "I agree with Prof, Billy. Better if we branch off from each other."

Prof nodded. "Possum's talking sense, Billy. You boys don't want to get mixed up in it. Robinson's got family back home. Sooner or later they'll trace out that he was up here in Wasted Gulch and put two and two together. You boys go on up into the mountains and find that there lake full of gold. Come down out of there rich as creases, I expect." He wiped himself off again. "Well, we best get moving before someone comes along and sees us. If anything comes out, we don't want anyone to recall seeing us here."

Billy was frowning and looking down at the dirt. "Prof, that's a fine thank you. We took all kinds of chances to save you. How many people would have jumped a fella holding two guns? Without us, you'd be laying in that hole instead of Robinson." I wished Billy would quit arguing about it. All I wanted to do was get away from that place.

"Oh, I'm mighty appreciative of what you boys did," Prof said. "I'll make it up to you someday. But it ain't safe now." He reached into his pocket and took out the wad of bills he'd taken off Robinson. Quickly he counted off ten dollars. Then he thought the better of it, shoved four back into the wad, and handed us the rest. "Here. Take it. A present from old Prof. Don't say I never did nothing for you. Now you two skedaddle out of here right quick. Best go off through the woods for apiece, so nobody coming along spots you near to here." With that, he turned and walked swiftly through the trees. In a moment we heard him shouting at the mules and the van rumbling back onto the highway.

"Billy, no use worrying it to death. He didn't want us along with him. Let's get out of here."

"Oh, I could see that. Blame him for a no-good skunk. He could of taken us if he wanted."

"But he didn't want to." I handed him the three bills Prof gave me. "Here, I don't want this stuff. He just gave it to us so's to make us part of it."

Billy took the bills. "I don't care about that," he said.

"Let's get out of here," I said once more. "What I reckon is, we climb down into that creek and walk along it a ways so's dogs can't pick up our scent."

He gave me a curious look. "Where'd you hear that one from?"

"James Fenimore Cooper. Some Indians did it to get away from Natty Bumpo."

We trotted back to the stream, pulled off our shoes, rolled up our pants, walked into the creek, and started upstream. There were stones underfoot which jabbed at the bottoms of our feet, and the water was cold and tugged at our legs. It took us a good twenty minutes of slogging through the current to cover half a mile. I wished I'd never heard of James Fenimore Cooper. Finally, we came to a bridge going overhead. We climbed out of the creek, dried ourselves off as good as we could with leaves, and went on back into Wasted Gulch.

We decided to keep away from the general store, for the fella there was bound to ask questions. We found another place and stocked up on enough stuff to last us a week—a sack of flour for biscuits, coffee, a tin of molasses, a bag of rice, and a bag of beans. Then we went across the street to the miners' supply store, where we bought a pan, a skillet, a couple of big tin spoons, a good-sized folding knife, some matches, and a little tin box to keep them dry in. In another place we bought two pieces of canvas big enough to lie on, some rope, and a couple of used army blankets for fifty cents each. When we heaped it up, I could see that just carrying it all was bound to make us sweat pretty good.

Billy still had a hankering to spend the night in the Majestic Hotel. "We ought to get a good night's sleep so as to start fresh in the morning."

Of course that wasn't it. He was just curious to know what sleeping in a hotel would be like—whether it would make us feel grand or something. All I wanted to do was get out of that blame town. To me, it smelled of death. I was having trouble understanding how I'd been in on killing somebody when we'd gone out there trying to stop a killing. Something to do with Billy, I reckoned. I'd gone along with him too much. Had since we were both little boys. It came from admiring him more than I should. I couldn't say that to Billy, though. He wouldn't understand it. So I said, "Billy, have some sense. We'd stick out like a sore thumb in that hotel. The sooner we get out of town, the better."

He could see that. So we divided up the supplies, bundled them up in the canvas tarpaulins, and slung them over our backs. They were heavy, all right. But we'd manage. And off we went in search of the golden lake at last. It made me feel good that we were finally on the right track.

There was a good-sized trail leading away from the town toward the mountains which went through a piece of brushy flatland. In a half hour we came to the gulch the place was named for. There was a wooden bridge across it, but since half the boards had fallen out of it and the timbers underneath were rotten, we scrambled down the side of the gulch, bringing stones and dirt after us, and then scrambled up the other side. Here the land sloped upward through a pine forest growing amongst rock outcroppings. Sometimes we could skirt around the rocks, but sometimes we had to climb over them. It was mighty hard work, hot and dirty, but I was glad of it, for it took my mind off Robinson stiffening up in that hole we'd dug for him. By the time it grew dark, we were both plenty tired and scratched up. We found a little mountain stream dashing down the rocks. We made a fire and cooked up some rice and biscuits. We didn't sit around long after supper, but curled up in our blankets. "If I knew exploring was such hard work, I'd of given it a second thought," Billy said.

"I guess we'll get used to it," I said. "I hope we spot that lake pretty quick, though."

We woke up at daybreak, kicked up the fire, made some coffee, and ate some cold biscuits and molasses. "We best follow alongside this stream," I said. "That lake's bound to have a stream coming out of it."

"How do we know if this is the right stream?"

"We don't," I said. "In fact, it probably isn't. I reckon a stream coming out of a lake would be bigger than this one. But it's the only one we got so far. Besides, if we stick with it, we'll have water."

We set off. We hadn't gone more than an hour when low clouds appeared in the east and the sky began to darken. Gradually they got thicker, and around noon, as close as we could figure time without the sun, it began to rain. We stopped, rigged up a tent with the ropes and the canvas, and huddled down inside it. "I didn't figure on rain," Billy said. "The way I pictured it, the sun was always shining and a nice breeze was blowing to keep us cool."

"Me, too," I said. "But it can't rain forever."

"It won't have to to discourage me. Two weeks'll be long enough."

The wind was strong, and the rain kept blowing in under the canvas. In an hour we were both soaked through and shivering. "There isn't any sense in this," Billy said. "We're drenched through, anyway; we might as well keep moving. That way at least we'll warm up."

We stayed warm all right, for the ground underfoot was soaked and slick as ice and we kept slipping and stumbling. The rain stopped around the middle of the afternoon, and by and by the sun came out, pale yellow and feeble. It wasn't going to dry off our clothes much. We stopped, found some dry firewood under a ledge, and got a fire going. Once the dry wood was burned we had to use wet wood, which steamed and flickered. We managed to boil up some rice and went to sleep naked, shivering, dozing, and waking. Finally, around three in the morning, Billy said, "Possum, I can't stand this; I'm coming in with you." We huddled together with both blankets and Billy's tarp on top of us. I was mighty glad to be warm for a change and went to sleep.

In the morning the sun came up bright and hot, which cheered us up a good deal. We got a good blaze going, cooked up a ton of biscuits, and sat there swabbing the molasses on them with the folding knife and washing them down with coffee. We strung a line from trees close to the fire and hung our clothes over it. While they were drying, I decided to ask Billy about some things.

"Billy, doesn't it bother you about killing Robinson?" I wasn't trying to change him or trying to argue him into seeing it my way. I was just trying to understand him better. We'd always taken each other for granted, the way you never give any thought to the air you breathe or the rain that falls on you from the sky. It was just there, and so was Billy.

He gave me a look. "Why? Does it bother you?"

"Yes." I looked at him and then away again. "Some."

"Not me," he said. "If he hadn't gone gunning for the Prof, it wouldn't have happened to him."

"Yes, but Prof started it when he got Robinson's little granddaughter killed."

"Oh, you can't blame that on Prof," Billy said. "He said himself he meant to warn them to take her to a doc."

"But don't you see, Billy," I said, looking at him, "it was all wrong from the start. If Prof hadn't been out there skinning people, both of them would be alive right now."

Billy shrugged. "How far back do you want to take it? If there weren't any such things as people, it wouldn't of happened, either."

"Aren't you even a little sorry?"

He lay down on his back where he could get the best use of the fire. "I don't reckon I'm the sort of type who gets sorry over things. It isn't my nature."

That was it, really: it was just his nature, and there wasn't much anyone could do about it. So I changed the subject to what we ought to do next.

For one thing, we'd lost our little stream. We were a good ways up. The woods had thinned out—mostly scrub oak and scrub pine, scraggly and no more than twenty feet high. Big pieces of rock stuck up everywhere among the trees, and because the trees were thin, the sun shone through pretty good. The mountain rose up above us like a wall. Directly ahead of us was a ravine full of boulders, sloping upward at a sharp angle. "Let's try the ravine," Billy said. "I reckon if we get up on some point where we could get a view of things, we might spot that lake."

It seemed like as good an idea as any. Our clothes were still damp, but we put them on, anyway, figuring they'd dry quick enough in the sun. We struggled up that ravine all morning. We came out onto a flat piece of ledge too stony for trees, but with enough dirt on it to grow a little grass. There was a pretty good view from up there across a saddle in the mountain, but no sign of a lake. We flung ourselves down on the grass to rest, and then Billy collected some firewood and got a fire going.

"Billy," I said, "we got to start going easy on the food. I figure we ought to skip lunch."

"Skip lunch, Possum? I'd rather be dead than skip lunch."

"Still, I reckon we better. The way I calculate, we haven't got enough for more than three days at most."

Billy frowned. "I'd of never come if I figured it meant skipping lunch. How long do you reckon it'll take to find that lake?"

"How do I know?" I said. "But the longer we can stretch out the food, the better chance we got of finding it." Then to encourage him I said, "Most likely we'll come across some blackberries or blueberries. There's bound to be fish in that lake, once we find it."

He gave me a look. "If you want to know what I think, Possum, I think we're a pair of fools off on a wild-goose chase. If we were with Prof right now, we'd be eating fried-egg sandwiches."

"Billy, Prof didn't want us to come with him."

174

"He'd of changed his mind after a while," Billy said.

"We got to give it a few more days."

"They're going to be mighty long days if we got to skip lunch."

We set off again, across the ledge and then on up the mountain face, looking for a good-sized stream that might be coming out of a lake. And we hadn't gone more than ten minutes when I realized I wouldn't have been able to trace my way back to the little ledge we'd rested on. "Billy, where *was* that ledge—that way, or over that way?"

He scratched his head. "Blamed if I know, now that you bring it up." It was just the way everybody said—those mountains twisted and turned so much you could get yourself lost in five minutes.

In the middle of the afternoon we found a stream. It was about five or six feet across, shallow, and running fast over the rocks. There were little fish in it, too. "That's a good sign, Billy. They must have come out of a lake, for they can't breed in a stream this fast." I had no idea if that was true, but I figured it'd encourage Billy.

For the next two days we followed that stream. My, it went every which way—around corners, cascading down cliffs, sliding through ravines, even wandering through small meadows tucked down in little mountain valleys. Every time we came around a corner I held my breath, praying that I'd see that lake. I wished

I could have enjoyed the scenery more, for it was mighty pretty—the sun slanting through the trees at sunrise and sunset, the rocky cliffs, red, blue, and yellow birds flashing through the trees, little meadows dotted with wildflowers; hawks floating high overhead, never moving their wings, but tipping this way and that to catch the wind. Oh, I could see it was pretty, but the way we were struggling over boulders, through briar patches and up cliffs, the prettiness of it didn't manage to come through.

We were parceling out the food pretty careful now, just a couple of biscuits and molasses for breakfast, water for lunch, and beans and rice for supper. Even so, on the third day, when we opened up our packs, we saw that we were down near to the end. "If we cut it in half, maybe we can hold out for another day," I said.

"If we cut it in half, Possum, it won't hardly be worth troubling with at all. You might as well stick to air and water."

"Maybe we'll come around a corner tomorrow and there that lake'll be. We'll need a meal to have the strength to haul all that gold off the bottom."

"We been at it six days, Possum. Tomorrow'll make a week. And on top of it, we don't know how long it's going to take us to get down out of here, with nothing but water and berries to keep us going. I reckon we better eat up what we got and call it quits."

"Just one more day, Billy." I knew there wasn't much hope in it anymore, but I knew I'd be sorry the rest of my life if I didn't push it as far as I could. "Please."

"All right, Possum. One more day. Only we eat the rest of the grub tonight. That way we'll get one satisfied night out of it, instead of two unsatisfied ones."

So we cooked up what was left and burned up the rice and bean sacks in the fire. In the morning we finished off the last of the molasses, buried the jar, packed up, and set off. The stream had narrowed down a little. It was headed up a long, gentle slope through a pine forest. It was an easy climb, or at least it seemed so after some of the places we'd climbed around and through and over. I guess we'd toughened up a little. You can get used to anything, they say, and we'd got used to banging our way around the mountains. Getting used to being hungry was going to be harder, I reckoned, but right then our stomachs were full.

Gradually the slope became rockier and steeper. The trees thinned out, so we were in the sun a lot, which got us sweating when it was still over in the east.

Then we came out of the trees. Ahead of us was a rocky ledge, covered with boulders, running up a steep angle. We stopped. "You think this is the top of the mountain, Possum?"

"Maybe right here it is. Seems like these mountains have got a lot of tops."

"Possum, let's call it quits. Every step upward is one more downward on an empty stomach. Let's turn around and head on back down."

He was right. I knew that. It was all over. We'd done our best, but it was over. But blame me if I could get myself to quit. That lake had to be out there somewhere. It just had to be. In my head I knew it probably wasn't, but no matter what was in my head, I still believed that lake was out there. "Billy, just a little more," I begged. "Just up to the top there."

"Possum . . ." He saw the look in my eyes. "All right. Up to the top. Then we take a look at the sights and head on down."

We picked up our bedrolls and began to climb the rocky ledge. In some places it leveled out and we could move along pretty easy; but in other places we had to pull ourselves along by grabbing on to whatever we could find—a piece of brush growing out of a rock, a crack in the ledge, a knob on a boulder. On up we went under the hot sun, a little breeze helping against the heat. Finally the ledge settled into a low curve, leveling out. And then we came over the top.

Down below was a meadow sitting in a bowl of the mountains, the sides covered with the same low pine trees we'd come out of. The meadow was thick with wildflowers, yellow, blue, white, and purple. Overhead a hawk glided easy in the wind. And in the middle of the meadow sat a little lake. All across its surface we could see spots of gold flickering and flashing. I threw my head back and laughed. Then I began to dance around on my toes. "We found it, Billy. I told you it was up here. We found it."

He whacked me on the back. "Come on, Possum, let's go."

We scrambled off the top of the mountain and ran down through the meadow toward the lake. I never felt so happy in all my life. I was just swollen with happiness. "Billy," I shouted, as we flew through the wildflowers, "we found it; we found it, Billy."

We came up to it. The lake wasn't more than a couple of hundred yards across. The banks of it sloped down fairly steep from the meadow. We crouched down in the grass and wildflowers beside it. Off toward the other side of the lake we could see gold flickering on the surface, but up close the gold disappeared. I stared down through the water. It was clear as could be. I could see fish easing around six feet below and, at the very bottom, rocks and weeds like green hair, hardly moving at all.

But no chunks of gold. I raised my head and looked across the lake to where the gold sparkled on the surface. "Maybe it's over there," I said. We stood up, trotted around the bank to the other side of the lake, and crouched down again to have a look. Now the gold flashes were back where we'd just come from; here the bottom was just rocks and weeds and fish swimming over them.

I looked at Billy and kind of whispered, "Billy, you don't believe the gold is just the sun shining on the surface, do you?"

He stood up and started unbuttoning his shirt. "I aim to find out." He threw his shirt and pants off. I knew I ought to undress and go into the lake with him, but I didn't have the heart for it anymore. It was only the sun flashing on the little waves stirred up by the light breeze. That's what Cook had seen, and that's all there was. Now it *was* over. I tipped my head down and squeezed my eyes closed, feeling like I'd lost the most important thing I ever had. It was a funny way to feel, for I never had that gold; but just being able to believe in it had made a whole lot of difference to me. Now I wished we hadn't come, for if we hadn't, I would never have known there wasn't any gold in that lake.

Then I heard a splash. I opened my eyes and looked out. There was a great ruffling in the water, and Billy's head popped up. "It's mighty cold, Possum. You coming in?"

"Maybe," I said.

He took a deep breath and plunged under the water. In a little bit he popped up again, waving something in his hand. "What's this, Possum? I got water in my eyes." He flung it onto the bank.

I picked it up and looked it over. "Nothing but a stone," I said. I dropped it into the grass.

Billy went on spluttering. "Possum, get my handkerchief out of my pants so's I can wipe my eyes."

I went over to where he'd dropped his clothes, picked up his pants, and reached my hand into his pocket. There was no handkerchief in that pocket, but there was something hard and slick. I pulled it out and let it lay flat on my hand. It was Pa Singletary's gold watch.

I spun around and held the watch up. "Blame you, Billy. Blame you for a rotten skunk."

"What's that, Possum?" He wiped his eyes with his hands. "What're you talking about?"

"The watch."

"Oh, oh," he said. He swam for shore and scrambled up onto the bank. "I didn't want you to see that, Possum. Give it to me."

Suddenly I'd had enough of Billy. Had my fill. The Singletarys were the only decent people I'd ever met in my life. Everywhere I looked there were people like Deacon whipping boys, the Prof skinning people with his elixir, the boys fighting and caterwauling and stealing from each other, Robinson burning to commit murder—everybody lying and cheating and stealing. Billy was one of them. It didn't matter that we'd slept in the same bed since we were a week old, didn't matter that we'd done everything together ever since. He was one of them.

Among them, the Singletarys shone out like a lantern in a dark forest. They were the best thing that ever happened to me, and what would they think of me now? I knew: they'd trusted me, liked me, and here

181

Billy had ruined it, for what would they think of me the minute Pa Singletary discovered that watch of his was gone? Just another worthless boy.

"Blame you, Billy," I shouted. "I don't ever want to see you again."

"Now hold it, Possum, I couldn't help myself. I told you I had to do something bad, but you wouldn't listen. Honest, I couldn't help it."

"I'm sick of you not helping things, Billy. I don't ever want to see you again."

"Possum, you don't mean that."

"Yes, I do." Then I jumped him. I just dove onto him, grabbed him around the neck, and started to squeeze. We went over in a heap, me on top of him, his fingers clawing at my hands, trying to break loose. But raging mad as I was, I was too strong for him. I went on squeezing.

"Possum," he gasped out in a raspy voice. "You're strangling me. You're going to kill me." He let go of my hands and began banging me around the head as hard as he could. I went on squeezing his neck, and all the while I was thinking, I can't believe this is me killing Billy.

Then he caught me a good one on the side of my head. For a minute I went dizzy, and my hands loosened up. He scrambled up from underneath me and stood in the grass and wildflowers, his fists clenched, in case I went for him again.

"You got yourself calmed down, Possum? I never saw you like that before."

I knelt up, panting, my head ringing from the punch he'd landed on it. I was glad I hadn't killed Billy, but I wasn't sorry I'd jumped him, either.

"That was the rottenest thing you ever did, Billy. You deserved to be strangled."

He turned his eyes away from me, toward the edge of the lake. "If you hadn't been so set on finding the gold, we wouldn't have gotten into this in the first place."

"Stop trying to throw everything off on somebody else, Billy. You can't go on doing that for the rest of your life."

Finally he looked at me. "You didn't have to strangle me for it."

"You deserved to be strangled. Those people were as nice as could be to us. The one thing Pa Singletary took any pride in, aside from Betty Ann, was that watch, and you stole it from him."

He didn't say anything and looked back down at the edge of the lake again. Maybe something was finally getting across to him.

"Can't you see it, Billy?" I said. "It isn't if *you're* bad or *you're* good. It isn't about *you*. It's what it does to other people."

Now he pulled himself up straight and stared at me. "I don't give a shoot what it does to other people. What have other people ever done for me?"

He had me there. I took a deep breath and tried to figure out where we were going with this. "Well, Pa Singletary was mighty kind to us."

"One person," he said

"And Betty Ann."

"Two, then."

"Three," I said.

"Who else?"

"Think, Billy, think."

He looked away again. "Oh," he said. Then he looked back at me. "We're kind of different aren't we, Possum."

He was looking kind of sad, and to tell the truth I was feeling sad myself. "Different in some ways," I said. "Probably the same in others."

"The same in others," he said, like he was trying to hold on to something.

All of a sudden I was completely tired out. I sat down amidst the tall grass and the wildflowers. "What do you reckon on doing once we get down out of here?"

He shrugged. "Try to find the Prof. His style suits me."

"Even after getting shot at and all?"

"I figure that was just an off chance. Most likely wouldn't happen again for a hundred years."

"You'll end up in jail, sure as shooting, Billy."

"Just you be sure to come and visit me," he said. He lay back in the grass beside me. "What do you figure on doing, Possum?"

"Well, first thing I got to do is bring that watch back to Pa Singletary."

"Something came out of it then," he said. "You got an excuse to go back."

"That's true," I said. I looked at him. "Don't start thinking that was why you stole it."

"You think you might stay there awhile?"

"I don't know," I said. "Maybe. For awhile, anyway. They sure could use some help." How would *Singletary* be for a last name? I tried it in my mind: Possum Singletary. Well, there was no telling how it would go. But it would be a nice change to be in a place where people were kind to each other on purpose.

It was going to be mighty strange going along without Billy. Sort of lonely at first, I figured. But I didn't see how it could be any other way. I sat up. "Billy, let's see if we can figure out a way to get a couple of those fish out of that blame lake."